S0-AGJ-360

San Jose
Public Library

FOR OVERTIME A CHARGE OF 5 CENTS A DAY

Careful usage of books is expected and any soiling,
damage or loss is to be paid for by the borrower.

A NEW AND
DIFFERENT SUMMER

A
NEW
AND
DIFFERENT
SUMMER

by Lenora Mattingly Weber

72253

THOMAS Y. CROWELL COMPANY / NEW YORK

Copyright © 1966 by Lenora Mattingly Weber
All rights reserved. No part of this book may
be reproduced in any form, except by a reviewer,
without the permission of the publisher.
Designed by Joan Maestro
Manufactured in the United States of America
Published in Canada by
Fitzhenry & Whiteside Limited, Toronto
Library of Congress Catalog Card No. 66-11951
ISBN 0-690-58040-1

To Lyle Liggett,
who first gave me the idea for this book

A NEW AND
DIFFERENT SUMMER

ONE

On a windy afternoon in early June when summer vacation was less than a week away, Katie Rose Belford halted outside John Quincy Adams High to wait for her friend Jeanie to join her.

Katie Rose breathed to herself, "Thank heaven, that's over."

She meant the school style show in which she had participated this afternoon in a "garden party" scene. She was still wearing the cream-colored dress of nubbly cotton lace over which she had labored for the past few weeks in second-hour sewing.

The wide purple belt felt uncomfortably snug over

the punch and cookies she had nervously gulped down at the reception following the fashion parade. She teetered on high heels as a gusty wind riffled her short dark hair and tossed it across her flushed cheeks. The pumps pinched her feet. They were a pair her mother had picked up at one of the church rummage sales she doted on. They had been white satin, but Katie Rose had sprayed them with instant shoe dye, not only to turn them the same purple shade as her belt, but so no one could *possibly* recognize them.

The wide glass doors fanned open again and again on clumps of departing students. What was keeping Jeanie Kincaid? She had stopped at the phone booth in the lower hall and said, "Wait outside for me, Katie Rose, while I phone Dad."

Katie Rose fingered the heavy necklace she was wearing. She would never have worn it except that her sewing teacher had insisted, "Now do wear some purplish beads to bring out the purple in your eyes." For the necklace too had a rather dubious history. One of Katie Rose's younger brothers had found it, broken and with a few beads missing, in the nearby city dump and had proudly raced home with it. "Why, you'd think they were amethysts," Katie Rose's mother had said happily. Enthusiasm was one thing the mother of the six Belford children possessed in abundance.

But supposing some girl had recognized that purple

necklace as one her mother had tossed in the discards?

Here came Jeanie now. She had not been in the fashion show for she was one of the sophomore reporters on the school paper and gave all her extra time to it. She pushed through the door wearing schoolday flats, brown skirt, and white blouse with smudges on its pocket from a ball-point pen. She was a small, elfin girl with cinnamon-brown hair and mischievous, twinkling eyes.

But this afternoon the twinkle was lacking. Katie Rose said, "I have to go past Wetzel's store to buy starch. Can you walk that far with me?"

Jeanie didn't answer, but juggled her load of books and fell into step with her. They passed loitering students on their way to the parking lot. And then Jeanie burst out, "Well, my phoning Dad was certainly a waste of time—and a dime. His answer was a big fat N-O on my going to the steak fry in the mountains this evening."

So that was the reason for Jeanie's mutinous look. She had told Katie Rose in French class this morning about the newspaper staff suddenly whipping up a steak fry in the foothills to celebrate their putting the final edition of the year "to bed."

"Ah, that's a shame, Jeanie. Why wouldn't your dad—?"

"Oh, the usual. He wanted to know who was going

to chaperone, and I told him Hig was going along."
Mr. Higgins was the young teacher-sponsor of the
paper. "But Dad seems to think a chaperone has to be
old and doddering. Then he wanted to know who I'd
be riding with—and I didn't know. It depends on who
can wangle cars. But no, he has to know the driver,
and see his brake and light sticker—"

"Maybe you could explain to your mother, and she
could—"

"Hah! I learned at an early age you couldn't play
one against the other. No, when Dad puts his heavy
foot down, it stays down."

This resentment of Jeanie's was something new.
Always before she had accepted her doctor father's
dictums with a good-natured shrug. "It's a wonder I
ever have a date," she would laugh. But, watchful
father or no, Jeanie Kincaid never wanted for dates.

They walked a block in silence, and again Jeanie
burst out angrily, "I don't know whether it's my phys-
ical safety or my morals he's so worried about. I wonder if he'd be that worried if I weren't adopted."

Katie Rose stopped on her wobbly heels and looked
at Jeanie in amazement. Her mind flashed back to last
September when she had first met Jeanie. It was on
registration day, and the two had walked from school
to the Kincaid home in Harmony Heights which lay
to the east of Adams High. Katie Rose had met Mrs.

Kincaid, a tall blond woman with friendly but grave blue eyes. She was such a contrast to Jeanie in height and coloring that when Katie Rose and she were opening Cokes in the kitchen, Katie Rose said, "You must look like your father."

Jeanie had answered casually, "I don't look like either of them. Dad's a big brawny Scotsman. I'm adopted. They took me when I was seven weeks old."

This whole school year, Katie Rose and Jeanie had been inseparable, sharing a locker, lunches, and hearts' secrets; Jeanie was the *only* one Katie Rose had told about her necklace being rescued from the city dump. But never once had Jeanie mentioned her adoption again. Katie Rose had all but forgotten it. She said now, "I didn't know you ever even thought about it—about being adopted."

"I don't brood about it, if that's what you mean. I couldn't love Mom and Dad more if they were my own. I hardly gave it a thought until the last year or two when I started dating. It's Dad being so eagle-eyed that makes me wonder what kind of stock I came from."

"But haven't your folks ever told you anything?"

"Sure, sure. I knew from the start I was adopted. They told me about how they loved me so much they wanted me for their own. Dad never wants to talk about it. He says that for an adopted child the book opens when she—or he—starts life with the foster parents. And he's right," she admitted loyally.

They had come to a street corner, and paused to let traffic go by. Jeanie repeated, "No, honest, I never gave it a second thought until lately. But just now when I called Dad at the office and he was so unbending, and kept saying he didn't like the idea of young folks being out on their own, I wanted to yell at him and say, 'Why? Is it because I come of trashy, immoral stock that you're afraid to trust me?' "

"Jeanie! You oughtn't to wonder things like that."

They crossed the street and started on before Jeanie flung out, "Why wouldn't I wonder? He's always made such a point of my telling the truth, and always accepting responsibility. Integrity—that's one of his favorite words. I just wish I knew that my mother *wasn't* some cheap little tramp that dumped me off at Mount Carmel."

"Mount Carmel? Was your mother working there that long ago?"

Jeanie nodded. "Yes, the day nursery started about then. And all I know is that someone left me there."

Mount Carmel was a day nursery at the end of the viaduct where working mothers left their babies in the morning and picked them up at the end of the work day. Jeanie's mother was one of its loyal volunteer workers. She put in a day or two each week.

They had reached Wetzel's Neighborhood Grocery, which could have been taken for a house with its porch across the front except for the bold brand names of coffee, bread, and creamery products vying with each other. The wind that was flattening their skirts was also rattling a tin sign that showed an up-tilted bottle, and the words, THE PAUSE THAT REFRESHES.

As they stopped at the foot of the steps to the made-over house to catch their breath, Katie Rose glanced at Jeanie's troubled face. "I know how you feel, Jeanie, about your dad's saying no to the flingding tonight. But I keep remembering that time when you and I wanted to ride up Pikes Peak with those boys in their old rebuilt stock car. And he said, 'Jeanie, I love you too much to say yes.'"

A crinkly smile erased the mutiny from Jeanie's face. "Yes, and he means it. Well, anyway I feel better for griping. What did you say you have to get here?"

"Starch. When I washed Ben's white jacket this morning there wasn't a drop of starch. Mom used the last of it to do up a stiff petticoat for her Gay Nineties costume."

A starched white jacket was a must for Ben, the oldest of the six Belford children, for his night job at a drive-in. And so were starched petticoats necessary for holding out the long, full skirts of the old-time dresses which Katie Rose's mother wore when she played the piano each night at Guido's Gay Nineties Club.

Katie Rose added, "Mom isn't the kind to make a list of things we run out of. She's not a bit organized about running a house. So now I'll have to hurry and make the starch and dip Ben's jacket in it and iron it for him to wear tonight."

"They have this spray starch now that you can spray on as you iron," Jeanie contributed.

Katie Rose stopped on the second step, and her words were like an explosion, "Not at our house. We never have anything up-to-date. Spray starch! It costs more than the kind you have to boil. And Ben is just like a watchdog of every nickel we spend—"

Jeanie laughed. "Watch it, chum. You're talking about my redheaded boy friend."

"I don't care if he is your boy friend. He's still old bossy Ben at our house."

"I like bossy men," Jeanie said. The twinkle was definitely back now. She said in a mimicking voice, "It isn't every high-school senior who feels responsibility for his widowed mother and his brothers and sisters. It's very commendable."

Katie Rose laughed ruefully at Jeanie's imitation of her father. Dr. Kincaid liked Ben Belford and never found fault with Jeanie's dating him.

"Okay, okay, you've got your gripes, Jeanie, ar
I've got mine. This is one," and she motioned to the
little store that was both store and living quarters for
the Wetzels. "I don't see why we can't buy at supermarkets like everybody else. But no, Mom is so small
town. She brings in cucumbers from Bannon for the
Wetzels to make dills, and cabbage for them to make
kraut. I tell you, Jeanie, it just turns my stomach the
way Mamma Wetzel always gives us their overripe
bananas without charging, and Papa Wetzel gives us
the bones he cuts hamburger off of and Mom makes
soup out of them. I hate this smelly old store—"

"Dad's crazy about their Liederkranz cheese,"
Jeanie put in.

Katie Rose returned to her grievances. "Spray
starch! Honestly, Mom is fifty years behind the
times. She still buys and cooks the way her mother did
back in Bannon."

Bannon was the small farming town, fifty-seven
miles from Denver, where Mother had grown up as
Rose O'Byrne. All the O'Byrne relatives still lived
there.

Katie Rose went on swiftly, "I just can't bear the
way Mom gets big sacks of whole wheat and white
flour and cornmeal and oatmeal from the Bannon mill
instead of in boxes at the supermarket."

"From the fellow who owns the mill—Leffingwell?

Ben says he's an old beau of your mother's and still—"

"Leff? Oh yes, everybody knows he still carries the torch for her." She dismissed that mention of romance and hurried on, "And Grandda O'Byrne brings us in bacon by the slab and whole hams we have to hack up with a saw. And every morning of the world Mom— no matter how late she's played the piano at Guido's— stirs up two big round knobby loaves of Irish bread. I live for the day when we can have sliced *white* bread like other people."

"I live for the day when I can say yes or no on my own. Golly, Katie Rose, wouldn't life be wonderful if we didn't have parents or grownups, and could live it our own way?"

"It'd be heaven on earth," Katie Rose agreed fervently.

They crossed the porch and opened the door into the store which rang a tinkling bell and always brought either Mrs. or Mr. Wetzel from their living quarters behind the store. Mamma and Papa Wetzel, the young Belfords called them—but not to their faces.

This afternoon Mrs. Wetzel was already behind the low counter of the small crowded store, engaged with what appeared at first glance to be a gaudily dressed girl with platinum blond hair. Katie Rose and Jeanie edged close to the rack of dry breakfast food, and smoothed back their blown hair.

It was the garish red, purple, and orange flowers in the dress of the girl at the counter that drew Katie Rose's closer attention to her. Why, she wasn't a girl at all. She must be as old as Katie Rose's own mother. And that teen-age hair-do didn't do a thing for her faded prettiness or for the hard lines in her face.

She wasn't a customer. She was trying to interest Mrs. Wetzel in handling some new kind of dog food, for she was displaying a tall stand-up ad showing a very pleased dog leaping for what resembled a rectangle of dog-burger. She was saying glibly, "It's going like hotcakes all over Arizona and California."

But she wasn't making much headway with the store owner. Katie Rose and Jeanie exchanged amused glances at the way Mrs. Wetzel's disapproving eyes swept over the saleslady. And no wonder! The splashy dress could have stood cleaning and pressing. The wearer was no taller than Jeanie, so that the turning up of a wide hem had been necessary in the skirt. But what a bundly job it was, with part of it already ripped out!

And when she bent her blond head to rummage for more advertising, the inch of brown hair roots disclosed that another bleach job was overdue. The hair close to her scalp was almost the same cinnamon brown as Jeanie's.

The creak of the big leather chair in the room behind the store was followed by the tap of a cane as a short, heavyset man limped into the store. Papa Wetzel smiled at the two girls. His eyes rested on Jeanie. "You're Dr. Kincaid's girl, aren't you? I told him I'd have his Liederkranz cheese in today. I'm looking for him to stop by."

A strange thing happened. The woman at the counter turned in such startled confusion that her tall stand-up ad fell to the floor. She stared at Jeanie, her lipsticked mouth gaping. Jeanie stared back in puzzled wonder. And then the woman scooped up all her display and literature and shoved it willy-nilly into a big pasteboard case. Without a word concerning the merits of her dog-burger, or even a good-by to the store proprietors, she scuttled out the door on the high runover heels of her sandals.

Katie Rose stepped toward the front of the store and watched her through the window as she climbed hastily into her car. The car somehow matched her own flashy but bedraggled pertness. It was a two-tone car, but what a combination of colors! Chocolate brown and an off-shade of pink, and both of them weathered and blotchy. The front and back fenders on the side visible to Katie Rose were badly crumpled.

Mrs. Wetzel's only comment was, "We don't have room for any new fancy dog food."

Jeanie told Mr. Wetzel that she would take home

some Liederkranz for her father. "I just talked to him, and he said his office was full and that he'd be late coming home."

Katie Rose bought her box of starch.

Outside, the girls paused again at the foot of the steps. Katie Rose asked, "Did you notice that dog-burger woman sizing you up, and then hustling out as though someone would bite her? Do you know her?"

Jeanie's elfin face puckered thoughtfully. "Not that I know of—and yet there was something about her—" She laughed. "You know what I'll bet? I'll bet she's been a patient of Dad's and still owes him money. She looks like the kind that'd be dodging bills. Wasn't she a hard-bitten number?"

Katie Rose nodded. "She's what Gran O'Byrne would call a brazen-faced trollop." She broke off to add under her breath, "Oh-oh! Speaking of brazen-faced— Here comes Rita Flood."

Next to Wetzel's store was a low, untidy shop with a sign, AL FLOOD, BODY AND FENDER WORK. The Flood family lived in a house, also low and untidy, behind the shop on the back of the lot which was cluttered with bent and rusty car parts. The ill-humored Flood parents screamed and fought with each other and with the children. The children screamed back at them, and fought among themselves and with any others in the neighborhood who crossed their paths.

Katie Rose's mother often said, "Those fightin' Floods—common as pig tracks. We'll give Al Flood any business we can," and though she had not a trace of snobbery, she always added, "but let's keep a safe distance from the whole family."

Keeping a safe distance proved a constant problem to Katie Rose. Rita Flood was one of her classmates at Adams High. Her attitude was that because she had gone to grammar school with Katie Rose she was one of her intimate friends. "It's that buddy-buddy act of hers that drives me mad," Katie Rose confessed to Jeanie.

Rita Flood stopped now as she reached Wetzel's steps. "Well, I wish you'd look! You're certainly all gussied up today, Katie Rose."

"Style show," she said briefly.

The dress which the wind flattened against Rita had once been white with oversize red polka dots. Careless washing had faded it until the red polka dots and white background were run together, and had shrunk it until it was well above her bare knees. Her face under her blowing hair was sharp and cocksure.

"Yeh, that sappy style show," Rita discounted. "Did you have a pattern for that dress?" Katie Rose nodded, and Rita promptly said, "Might be I'll borrow it and make me one just like it to wear on a juicy date."

Of all the gall! You'd think she'd say, "I'd like to borrow it," or "Would you mind if I made a dress like yours?" The truth of the matter was that Katie Rose did mind. She had bought the material with her baby-sitting money, planning that this dress would be her best for summer and for school events next term. And she certainly didn't relish the thought of Rita Flood flipping about in one just like it.

Rita Flood studied the dress with greedy eyes. She even felt the material and lifted up the hem. "Lined, all but the sleeves, huh? How many yards of cotton lace did you buy for it?"

"Two and a half, I think. Depends on how long you make the sleeves."

"I could make it out of *two*," Rita bragged. "I'll bet you spent weeks and weeks making it in school. I could make it in an afternoon, easy."

Jeanie put in, "That's what you think. Not when you slave over putting in a lining without a pucker."

But Rita had the last word as she went up the store steps. "Who needs a lining? All you need is a slip. Those teachers at Johnny Q lie awake nights thinking up ways to make you kill time."

Wetzel's door closed behind her. Katie Rose's and Jeanie's eyes met in helpless exasperation. No words were necessary. They had said them all before. Katie

Rose had explained to Jeanie the first day of school last September, "I don't dodge Rita because of her messy folks or that messy house or the way she dresses—or even because her brothers are always in and out of the Reform School. I feel sorry for her—"

"You can feel sorry for someone without liking her," Jeanie had said in understanding. "She's the kind that if you gave her an inch, she'd take three miles."

Jeanie said now with a meaningful laugh, "If I were you, I'd lose that pattern."

"I really don't know what I did with it." Katie Rose's eyes dropped to the box of starch in her hand. "Ben's jacket is calling. I must tear—as fast as I can in these heels."

"Wait a sec. Can you think of anything to rhyme with 'pre*sent*'?"

Katie Rose stared blankly for a moment. "Oh, for your *pome*." Tomorrow, the outgoing editor of the school paper was to be presented with a pen and pencil set by the staff. Jeanie, who had a knack for writing verse, had been designated to write one to be read for the occasion. "De*scent*, predica*ment*—no, that's not so good. La*ment*?"

Jeanie giggled ruefully, "I *lament* that while the gang is making merry at their steak fry, I'll be sitting home writing verse."

They separated. Jeanie turned east toward the new addition known as Harmony Heights, and to a low ranch house with a pink tiled roof and pink front door, and a wrought-iron sign in the front yard that said, SCOTT W. KINCAID, M.D. Katie Rose turned west to the older district which some wit had once labeled Hodgepodge Hollow, and to a shabby two-story brick on the corner, and the bicycles of the three youngest Belfords decorating the lawn.

TWO

Katie Rose was still a half-block away from the Belford red brick house on Hubbell Street when she saw the dusty pickup with a Bannon license parked at the curb to the side of the house. That meant she would find Grandda O'Byrne at home. He was a builder in Bannon, and his pickup as usual was loaded with tools and lumber.

Simultaneously, the gate to the picket fence that enclosed their back yard was banged open and three figures in Levi's and T-shirts came racing toward her, yelling through the wind as they did, "Guess what, Katie Rose? Guess what?" A brown-and-white dog cavorted joyfully about them in wild self-importance.

These were the three youngest of the six Belford children—the ones who loved nothing better than poking through the city dump and bringing home the "treasures" they found. At first glance they could be taken for a set of triplet boys. It took a second look to see that one of them, in spite of the boy's haircut, tanned snub-nosed face, and grimy hands, was a girl. It would take a third glance for a stranger to realize that the one with a sober and sweet smile was younger than the harum-scarum twins, Matt and Jill.

The twins were going on twelve. Brian, the youngest, was going on eleven. The family always lumped the three together as "the littles."

By the time they reached Katie Rose, they were shouting out the answer to their "Guess what?" It was, "Whatta you know—Mom's going to Ireland with Gran."

Katie Rose stopped at the curb in such surprise that again she lost her balance on her high heels. "Mom's going to Ireland with Gran?" she repeated, and then automatically, "Jill, wipe the jam off your face."

Jill made a hasty swipe across her face with the tail of her T-shirt. Brian added gravely, "They have to go because poor Nellie's on her deathbed over there."

Poor Nellie? That would be their great-aunt Nellie, Gran O'Byrne's older sister who was only a name to the young Belfords—a name on a battered box from Cork, Eire, containing heavy hand-knit sweaters. "But why does Mom have to go to Ireland with Gran?" Her mother, as Katie Rose knew, had been born in Bannon and had never laid eyes on this old lady named Nellie Callanan.

"Because Gran's afraid to go all by her own self," Jill said readily. She was the self-appointed spokesman for the three. "Grandda said it was his place to go with her, but he's building a new wing on the schoolhouse in Bannon and can't leave, and so he said he was willing and glad to pay Mom's plane fare to go with Gran."

"Over and back," put in Matt. "Because the school has to be done by September, and he said he'd be money ahead to pay Mom's way."

"They're going to take poor Nellie a hot-water bottle," added Brian.

Katie Rose quickened her steps through the picket gate, and latched it against the wind that was banging it back and forth. With the littles still talking excitedly, she went in the side door at the back which opened into the dining room and was only a few steps from the kitchen. Once inside, she lost no time in bending over and pulling off the pinching slippers.

Her younger redheaded sister Stacy was refilling the teapot, and she too was bubbling over with the news. "You're just in time, Katie Rose. Gran came in with Grandda. Ben is home. And we're all at the dinette table, holding a constellation about Mom's taking off for Ireland with Gran."

"Con-sul-ta-tion," Katie Rose corrected. It seemed to her that she went through life not only saying to one of the littles, "Wipe the jam"—or cocoa or gravy—"off your face," but correcting Stacy for her manhandling of words. You'd think a freshman in high school would know the difference between *constellation* and *consultation*. Katie Rose added, "A constellation is a group of stars."

"Well, aren't *we*?" Stacy returned with a blithe toss of her pony tail. It took more than a correction to down Stacy.

The dinette, once the back porch, was off the kitchen. From it came a booming voice with a trace of Irish brogue, "Here's our blackbird, and looking lovely as springtime in her fancy togs."

"Fashion show at school, Grandda," Katie Rose said as she bent to kiss his ruddy, weathered cheek.

He always called her blackbird because she was the only black-haired one in the family. His own hair was a red that had deepened, not grayed, with the years.

Mother had inherited it. She had the transparent, glowing skin to go with it. Add to that, sparkling blue-green eyes and a spilling-over laugh, and it was no wonder people always said, "She looks so young to have children in high school." She was also loving, impulsive, and tempery, and not as orderly as Katie Rose would have liked.

Ben too had the O'Byrne red hair along with Grandda's thin, rugged face and tall figure. Stacy's pony tail that bobbed at the back of her head was more of an auburn-blond. The littles all had curly hair the golden brown color of cornflakes.

Gran O'Byrne sat next to Ben at the dinette table. She was a small sparrow of a woman who, as long as Katie Rose could remember, wore her gray hair in a bun, and button-down-the-front dresses.

She said to Katie Rose now, "Oh, child, put an apron on over that light dress. A bit of blackberry jam would be the ruin of it."

"Sit down, Katie Rose," Ben ordered. "We're just hashing over about how we could get along if Mom goes to Ireland with Gran."

"I'll listen. But I have to starch your jacket and hang it out in the wind for a few minutes."

She did put on an apron. The starch-making didn't take long, what with the teakettle full of boiling water. She thinned the hot starch with cold water and plunged the jacket into it.

Stacy took it from her when it was wrung out. "I'll hang it on the line for you." She added with her roguish grin, "I'm being nice to you because I'm bustin' to borrow your new creation. I've even poured your tea. Sit down and drink it."

Gran turned troubled eyes to Katie Rose and began explaining in disjointed fashion, "I was just saying— Sure, I could never live with myself if I didn't go. Nellie was good to us when we were growing up—but I'm such a helpless old thing when it comes to traveling—I wouldn't be knowing which plane to get on. But the parish priest wrote me that Nellie was down in bed—she was asking for me, he said. Mayhap I should have gone before—it doesn't seem right for poor Nellie lying there on her deathbed and no one to do for her. But I'd be frightened to go alone—and I thought if only your mother could manage—"

Jill said, "I should think Aunt Kitty in Bannon could go with you, Gran."

Mother turned distracted eyes to the three littles perched as they always were on the sacks of flour and meal ranged along the dinette wall—those sacks that Katie Rose resented so. Mother often left the flour sifter in one, and she said now, "If one of you are sitting on my sifter, I'll bash it over your head."

Her threat left them untroubled. Jill went on, "Aunt Kitty's only got one child to leave, and Mom's got all of us."

"Kitty!" Grandda grunted around his pipe.

"Wurra, wurra—one lone child or no, she could never leave. Your Uncle Tim has to have his hot meal at noon when he's working."

Gran looked helplessly at Mother. "Even so, I'd rather go with you, Rose, my own," she said like a child.

"What do you think about my going, Ben?" Mother appealed to him.

Ever since Father's death three years ago, Mother leaned heavily on Ben—Ben, the protector, the watchdog of the family. There was a strong and loving bond between them; Ben worried about Mother's working so hard, and Mother worried for fear Ben would be "an old man before his time."

His deep blue eyes were thoughtful. "I don't see why you couldn't go, angel. I think you ought to. Now when is Guido planning on closing the Gay Nineties for remodeling?"

"At the end of next week. He's adding on a banquet room, and redecorating. He'll be closed for a month—"

Grandda, the builder, interrupted, "If he can get all that done in a month, I'll eat my hat."

"How long will you be gone?" Katie Rose asked.

Grandda answered, "That's hard to say. A month, maybe six weeks. I doubt if Nellie's on her deathbed, but someone has to go over and arrange for her being cared for. What about you, blackbird? Couldn't you hold the place together while your mother's gone?"

"Of course I could." And her heart lifted into her throat as she thought, Here's my chance to show them all how a house ought to be run.

Mother threw back her head and laughed. "Oh, she could—she could, indeed. She could do a better job than I do. At least that's what she's forever telling me."

They all chuckled at that. As though the very idea of a sixteen-year-old girl thinking she could run a house and feed six hungry children better than her mother was a big joke.

Let them laugh their heads off, Katie Rose thought. If I were running this house, we wouldn't all be crowded here in the dinette having tea with thick chunks of Irish bread. Everybody wouldn't be dipping into the blackberry jam that Liz is always bringing or sending in from Bannon. (Liz was another of their Irish relatives.) No, sir, we'd be having tea in the living room with little thin cucumber sandwiches made of *white* baker's bread.

The talk had now got down to details of the trip; the smallpox shots and passports. There always seemed to be a family connection in key spots, and Grandda mentioned a Callanan at the Federal Building who would rush through their passports. Katie Rose listened to the talk, to the flap-flapping of Ben's white jacket in the wind, but she was already planning that when she took over, those offending sacks of flour and meal would be no more. Yes, and she'd let down the bamboo curtain between dinette and kitchen so it wouldn't seem like eating in the kitchen. . . .

The talk veered off the trip to Ireland. Stacy came in for Grandda's scolding. "What's this I hear about you, missy? That the Sisters at St. Jude's only passed you on condition that you go to summer school? And what was the cause of that now—too much basketball, and lallygaggin' with the boys, I've no doubt?"

"I passed everything but Latin and lit. Lit was just awful. All those reports on drippy books like *Withering Heights* and—"

"*Wuth*ering," Katie Rose corrected.

"Well, it *withered* me," Stacy grumbled. To escape further reproaches, she leaped to her feet. "I'll get Ben's jacket. It ought to be dry enough to iron." And when she came dashing back with it, she nudged Katie Rose with a whispered, "Get them talking about something else."

Katie Rose did. She said, "I won't be ironing a white jacket for Ben much longer."

That turned the conversation to Ben's summer job. After graduation next week from Adams High, he was quitting as sandwich man at the drive-in to go to work for a construction company that did road-building. Grandda, with his building contacts, had "put in a word" for his grandson. "It's good pay, Ben," he commented now, "but ah, lad, the sore muscles you'll have at the start."

Ben only grinned. "I can take it."

The littles, having heard enough of grown-up talk, now took themselves off to spread the news that Mother was going to Ireland.

There was a moment's waiting lull in the dinette until the clatter of departing bicycles told them that the three were well out of earshot. Then Grandda said, "So you had the littles give up their paper route, Rose?"

For over a year Matthew and Brian—and of course Jill—had scrambled out of bed at five, and untied the heavy bundle of papers which earlier had been thumped on the Belford porch. They folded, rubber-banded them, packed them in bags on their bicycles, and set out to throw them at doorways.

Mother answered, "Oh, Da, it wasn't so bad until the *Call* did away with dropping the bundles off for the carriers. They had to go to a sub-station to get them and fold them—"

Stacy said feelingly, "Those other kids were all older and bigger than our littles—and all of them tough as a two-bit steak. Every blessed morning our littles came home so battered and bruised—why, we couldn't even keep enough Band-Aids."

Grandda said with a downtwisted smile, "Our three fightin' tigers were never above starting a scrap."

Katie Rose contributed, "A boy pulled the sleeve clear out of one of Jill's sweaters."

"She bit him on the ear," Stacy finished proudly.

Gran shook her head and made tch-tching sounds.

"That Jill!" Mother exclaimed worriedly. "She doesn't know yet that she isn't a boy. It was because of her—and what some boy at the station said to her—" A flush suffused her face at memory of it. "I couldn't even repeat it."

Katie Rose, whisking her iron over a sleeve of the white jacket, blushed herself as she thought back to it. They had all been at the breakfast table when Jill quoted that shocking remark a boy, known only as Tex, had made to her, and asked innocently what it meant.

Mother had choked on her coffee, and turned stricken eyes to Ben. Ben had said instantly, "That does it! Jill, you've had your last morning of mixing with those hoodlums. You, Matt, and Brian, finish out the month. And tomorrow, you tell your boss you're quitting your route the first of June."

"Saint Brigid have mercy!" Gran murmured now, and Grandda added, "The little money they made wasn't worth all the squabbles and hard work."

Gran and Grandda knew how the littles' net profit was never what it was supposed to be. Customers moved away without paying. Once Matt's hurled paper missed the porch and hit a picture window, and the replacing of it ate up a month's profit. Besides, as Ben said, they had their three bicycles to support.

He said now, "They can cut a few lawns this summer."

"Can't you get that spalpeen of a Jill into a dress?" Grandda chided. "Has she no vanity?"

"The other girls got it all," Ben said. "They've got it to spare."

"They have, they have," Grandda smiled, looking fondly at Katie Rose and Stacy, "and they've a right to it. I wouldn't give a cherub's apron for a woman without it."

Gran was still worrying about Katie Rose's cream-colored lace dress. "Hadn't you better be after changing out of it, Mavourneen?"

"I'm going to wear it this evening, Gran. I'm baby-sitting at the McHargs' while they go to dinner and some golf celebration at the club. It isn't like other baby-sitting jobs, so I won't get it dirty there." She didn't add that she wanted to show it off. Vanity! Vanity!

Ben said, "If Katie Rose keeps house while Mom

is gone, she'll turn our house into the McHargs'. That's all we hear from her. 'Mrs. McHarg always has flowers on the table.' 'Mrs. McHarg never has boiled cabbage.' 'Mrs. McHarg keeps a grocery list so she never runs out of anything.' "

Mother's spilling-over laugh was rueful. "That paragon of a Mrs. McHarg! God save us, I could never live up to her."

But I can, and I will, Katie Rose at the ironing board vowed. I'll run this house and serve meals in the modern, up-to-the-minute way. I'll buy all those delectable packaged foods at the supermarket.

Grandda unfolded his tall sinewy length from the dinette bench. He held out a hand to help his wife up, and said as he always did, "We'd better be heading for home, Mrs. O. We'll be in touch with you by phone, Rose. You talk over your leaving with Guido tonight. Might be you can get off the day of Ben's graduation. We can't miss seeing our Ben in cap and gown."

THREE

Katie Rose had only time to put Ben's ironed jacket on a hanger and slide her feet into the purple pumps when Mr. McHarg came for her.

He was a forceful but genial young executive who liked to call Katie Rose the *femme fatale* of South Denver and laugh to see her blush. He noticed her fashion-show costume the minute she stepped out the front door, and gave an appreciative whistle.

From the time Katie Rose was fourteen and began her baby-sitting at the McHargs', the job had never been a chore but a delight. They were like a story-book family—Mother, Father, and two pretty, well-dressed little blond girls, all living happily in a story-book house.

With expert ease Mr. McHarg whisked the car into his driveway beside a white clapboard house with turquoise blue shutters in Harmony Heights. He and Katie Rose walked through the patio and into the gleaming kitchen.

Mrs. McHarg, already dressed, was waiting for them there.

She was young and attractive. She was never flustered, never raised her voice to the well-mannered little Diane and Debbie. You'd never hear *her* say, "If you sit on my flour sifter, I'll bash it over your head." (But then she'd never have a sifter in a sack of flour in her dinette.)

She always found time to take courses in dressmaking, child psychology, flower arangement, and meal-planning, and she did everything with deft capability. She was Katie Rose's idol.

And she always looked just right. This early evening she was wearing a rose dress of sheer wool with miniature golf-ball buttons. The matching sweater was over her arm. *She* would never buy haphazard items of clothing at rummage sales as the Belford mother did.

She showed Katie Rose the glass baking dish with rolled crepes, all ready for the oven. The salad vegetables waited shiny and crisp on the sink drainboard. The dining table was already set. Even as Katie Rose saw that there were *four* lacy table mats, *four* Mexican blue water glasses, Diane said, "Perry will be here too. He's our cousin. And I get to introduce him to you because I'm a first-grader and Debbie is only in kindergarten."

Mr. McHarg was saying, "Let's go, Carol, so we can catch the tail-end of the tournament. Come on— come on."

Mrs. McHarg said from the doorway, "Goodness, I forgot with this man hurrying me— Yes, Perry Mc-Harg, Mac's cousin, is here. He came up from Phoenix to take a workshop at the university on Hotel and Restaurant Management. He'll be home for dinner."

Mr. McHarg called back as he opened the car door for his wife, "Don't go captivating the poor guy, Katie Rose. Leave him enough mind for comparing dish-washers, and learning how to turn a chuck roast into a standing rib."

The car had no sooner left the driveway than Katie Rose asked the little girls, "How old is your cousin?"

"Nineteen, going on twenty," Diane said. "He's in college."

Going on twenty? Maybe he'd think a girl going on seventeen beneath his notice. Yet she was glad she'd worn her fashion-show dress, high heels, and purple necklace. And a college student from Phoenix would have no way of knowing the necklace had been rescued from the city dump.

With an added tingly excitement, Katie Rose turned her attention to the dinner. The efficient Mrs. Mc-Harg had left nothing to doubt. Here on the built-in desk between kitchen and utility room was the menu for the first Thursday in June:

> *Chicken and mushroom crepes*
> *Buttered broccoli (frozen)*
> *Tossed salad with Roquefort dressing*
> *Blueberry muffins (package mix)*
> *Ice cream with slivered almonds*

Katie Rose had told the family at home how each Monday morning Mrs. McHarg went through her week's menus, consulted the attached recipes, and made out her shopping list. "And she jots down exactly how long each meal takes to prepare."

"For the love of heaven," Mother had snorted. "Sounds like the Union Pacific running on a time-table."

Comparisons! Always comparisons when Katie Rose stepped into this roomy and ultra-modern ranch house. Here the sideboard was graced with a piece of drift-wood holding a fruit arrangement of apples, peaches, red cherries, and pale green grapes spilling over them. Katie Rose thought of their cluttered sideboard at home.

Here the polished surface of the dining table showed through the lacy mats of yellow woven straw. On their dining table at home Mother's old portable sewing machine sat, crowded by schoolbooks and the mending she was always going to get to. The Belford meals, except for holidays and company dinners, were eaten at the long dinette table with its benches on three sides.

Katie Rose washed her hands before mixing the tossed salad. Comparisons again! The McHarg bathroom with its array of colored towels was like a rainbow. She knew by now that the blue towel set was for Diane, the pink for Debbie. The forest green ones were for Mr. McHarg, the orchid for Mrs. The fluffy yellow ones were for guests; they even proclaimed it with WELCOME on one, TO OUR on the second, and HOUSE on the third. These of course were used by the as yet unseen Perry McHarg.

A far cry from the Belford upstairs bath and the limp towels anyone and everyone grabbed for.

Perry McHarg drove up in his station wagon just when the timer gave an announcing ping that the muffins were ready to take from the oven. He was duly and primly introduced to Katie Rose by Diane.

All the while Katie Rose dislodged the small muffins onto a napkin-covered plate, she was trying to fit him into some category.

He was not the college-athlete type, even though, like Mr. McHarg, he was broad of shoulder and had a healthy ruddiness. Not the studious grind either, even though he wore glasses. The dark rim at the top emphasized his straight heavy eyebrows. And not a smoothie with a wise-cracking patter. He puzzled Katie Rose.

His thoughtful interest in the food puzzled her even more. He said after his second bite of the rolled crepes, "Canned mushrooms."

"It's canned chicken too," Diane said. "Mother says it's easier."

"It's more expensive though."

He buttered a blueberry muffin, and lifted his opaque hazel eyes to Katie Rose. "A ready-mix. Is this what the package makes—eight small muffins?"

For heaven's sake!—but not one word about the purple beads doing things for her eyes. Maybe he thought she was just a mill-run, high-school sophomore baby-sitter.

She said, "I'll be a junior next year, and the drama teacher told me—" Watch it, she warned herself. Remember your besetting sin is trying to impress people. Besides, what do you care whether this square-faced McHarg cousin notices you or doesn't?

Yet she couldn't help feeling grateful when Diane said, "Katie Rose can sing and dance better'n anybody in the whole world. Once she sang a song on St. Patrick's night and a man told her he'd give a hundred dollars to have what she sung on a record. It was about a heart in two little hands—tell him about it, Katie Rose."

She said with what she hoped was seeming modesty, "It's an old Irish ballad—'You Hold My Heart in Your Two Little Hands.' Everybody in our family sings. I have an uncle who says that singing comes as natural to an O'Byrne as howling to a cat."

His smile changed the whole alert, sober cast of his face. "I can't sing for sour apples. I'm the rooted-to-the-ground type," he said.

The smaller Debbie, not to be outdone, contributed, "Katie Rose has a beau, and he takes us for rides in his little-bitty car. He's our favorite. He calls her Petunia because she's so pretty."

His laugh was hearty too. "What is this—the Katie Rose publicity department?"

Yet the build-up must not have registered. For he stood up and said, "Just skip me on the dessert. I want to run back to school and check over some freezers."

"Is that what you study in this hotel course?"

"It's part of it. We study nutrition and foods and

equipment. We try out and compare everything from shortening to swimming pools and cooling systems. My folks own a motel in Phoenix, and we're about to add a swimming pool and dining room. On borrowed money, so that's why life is real and life is earnest."

Yes, his smile did reach out to her. She wished life weren't so real and earnest so that he could take time to notice the girl under her fashion-show costume.

She couldn't resist saying, "My mother is planning to fly to Ireland." She said it as casually as though her mother were in the habit of flitting back and forth to Europe. "And I'm to look after the house and family while she's gone. I'm going to do it the way Mrs. McHarg does because Mom—well, she's one of these old-fashioned cooks—"

"How many are there in your family?"

"There're six children."

"And your father? Is he going with your mother?"

"My father's dead."

Diane put in, "Katie Rose's mother plays the piano and sings songs every night out at a place where the waiters have great big mustaches. What do they call it, Katie Rose?"

"Guido's Gay Nineties," she said briefly.

"And so you're going to copy Carol's—Mrs. McHarg's—way of buying and cooking?" he asked, and looked at her as though he were really seeing her for the first time.

"Oh yes! I'm going to copy all her menus and recipes tonight. I can hardly wait to have things different at our house." She sang out happily, "There'll be some changes made."

He continued to look at her as he slowly zipped up his briefcase and started for the door. He turned with his hand on the door to ask, "Would you go to lunch with me some day at the Golden Slipper?"

It all but took her breath away. The Golden Slipper was the very swanky dining room at a very swanky new motel. "Oh yes." And then, not wanting to sound too eager, "I can manage to get away at noontime. There'll just be the littles and Stacy to fix lunch for because my brother Ben will take a lunch on his construction job."

His smile was still thoughtful. "I'll give you a ring," he said, and was gone.

Well, well! So all his interest wasn't given over to food and cooling systems after all.

Dinner over, she put the dishes in the dishwasher, planning ahead to that luncheon at the Golden Slipper. Just wait till she told Jeanie she would be lunching with a man of the world!

But she had other things to think about. While the little girls watched their favorite TV show, she sat down at the kitchen desk and copied Mrs. McHarg's menus and recipes. She had eaten many meals here in the past two years, all balanced, delicious, and pleasing to the eye. On several occasions when she had stayed overnight in the guest room, she had breakfasted with them.

The McHargs breakfasted on fruit juice, a choice of the dry breakfast foods that came in a six-pack, and perhaps a poached egg on a toasted English muffin, or triangles of cinnamon toast hemming in sausage links.

Belford breakfasts were invariably a big kettle of the oatmeal that came from the Bannon mill, thick slices of bacon hacked off a great slab. And eggs—oh, those awful eggs that also came from Bannon, not in egg cartons, but wrapped in the thin pages of a mail-order catalog and packed in shoe boxes. A few were always cracked on the trip in. The paper stuck to them, and the eggs stuck together. They too were on her do-away-with list.

She got up and glanced in the McHarg refrigerator. Beautiful! Butter in neat cubes, bacon in flat packages, clean white eggs in their own niches. Neat stacks of brown'n serve rolls and coffee cakes ready for the oven.

That's the way the Belford refrigerator was going to look, once Mother took flight to Ireland and Katie Rose was at the helm.

She had copied June menus up to the second Friday of the month. She was writing:

Shrimp salad in avocado halves
Frozen french fries
Frozen spinach soufflé

when the TV watchers in the living room gave a glad shriek, "Katie Rose, he's here. Miguel is here." Their program dwindled to unimportance with his arrival. Each one clung to a hand as he came into the kitchen.

"Hi there, Petunia. I stopped at your house and they said you were here."

Miguel should have been called *Michael*. But he had come up from Mexico to go to Adams High with a transcript made out for Miguel, and the name had stuck to him.

He was carrying a camera in a scuffed leather case. "I had to show you what Pop sent me from Alaska." His writer father, also Michael Parnell, was in Alaska gathering material for a book while Miguel lived with his grandparents and went to Adams High. "It's a Leica, Petunia. Pop said he was through taking pictures for his book. This is the kind professional photographers use. I remember when he bought it in Germany. Isn't it a beaut?"

One of the little girls said, "We thought maybe you'd take us for a ride in your little-bitty car."

He looked down at their wistful faces from his lanky height. "Petunia, why don't you take them? I want to phone a photographer I know. He told me once that sometimes he needed help on a picture-taking assignment. Is that all right, petty-dolls?" He handed Katie Rose his keys.

The little-bitty car was a five-year-old blue Triumph with white sidewall tires. On his seventeenth birthday in April, Miguel's father had sent him the money to pay the difference in trading in his very battered and ancient Mercedes on it. "Gramps can't stand the sight of it," Miguel had told Katie Rose. "He calls it my wheelbarrow."

Katie Rose loved the TR. She loved driving it. This evening she drove Diane and Debbie through the park and back, and Diane sighed as she climbed out, "When I get as big as you are, I'm going to have a beau with a TR too."

There was no use trying to explain to them that Miguel wasn't *exactly* her beau. He was like one of the family, bobbing in and out of the Belford house. He seemed just as happy taking Stacy to one of her basketball games, or Mom across town to one of those church rummage sales she delighted in, as taking Katie Rose to a school hop. He was just Miguel with his heart-warming chipmunk grin, his straw-colored hair that disdained a part, and his shirts that never stayed tucked in.

Certainly Katie Rose need have no guilt stirrings for looking ahead to lunching with an enigmatic college man named Perry McHarg.

Miguel had lined up a job while they were gone. His photographer friend had said yes, he'd be glad for some help a week from Saturday. A new shopping center was opening that day. "It's called Maplewood Mart and it's way out toward Derby. They've cooked up an advertising scheme to have pictures taken of the shoppers as they come out, and then they'll run, say, ten or twelve in the paper. And the person who finds his picture can bring it back and get five-dollars' worth in trade. How'd you like to go with me, Petunia—you and Jeanie?"

"I'd love to. I love supermarkets. I'm copying Mrs. McHarg's menus and recipes. Because when Mom goes to Ireland with Gran, I'll be running the house."

"Run it the way your mother does. That's the kind of a house I like. Always plenty to eat," he gave her his urchin grin, "for a hungry guy that drops in."

She wouldn't argue with him. She wouldn't even mention that there was to be no more Irish bread for him to wolf down with big cups of tea.

He didn't stay long. He wanted to buy some film

for his camera at Downey's Drug on the Boulevard.

Diane and Debbie's bedtime was at eight. They never begged to stay up later. They got into their ruffly baby-doll pajamas, and brushed their teeth without having to be reminded. They only asked, as they always did, for Katie Rose to sing them Brahms' "Lullaby" as they snuggled into their twin beds.

Katie Rose had copied menus and recipes for all of June and part of July by the time the McHargs returned. Mr. McHarg said, "I suppose you sent Perry off in befogged dreams."

That'll be the day, she thought. But he *had* asked her to lunch at the Golden Slipper.

It was eleven o'clock by the time Mr. McHarg took her home and walked her to the front door. She felt her usual letdown at coming into the shabby, cluttered Belford house after an evening at the McHargs'. The shower was running in the newly installed bath under the stairs, which meant that Ben was home after his night's stint at the drive-in.

Stacy came in from the kitchen, taking alternate bites out of the apple tart in one hand and a piece of ham in the other. For a slender girl of fifteen and a half with a lilting voice and light dancing feet, Stacy had an amazing appetite. She often giggled ruefully, "I've lost more boy friends because I eat too much. They stop and expect me to order a Coke, and does it ever throw them when I want a double-malt and hamburger."

The littles were still up. "You ought to be in bed," scolded Katie Rose. "The McHarg girls go without being told."

"Oh them!" sneered Jill.

"We've been out collecting," Matt defended, and Jill added, "Five people still owe us for their papers. And one of them is never, never at home—and she owes us for *two* months."

Mother came in with glad excitement coating the weariness she always felt after an evening of piano-playing and singing. "I talked to Guido about leaving, and it's all right with him," she called through the house.

She was dressed in keeping with the Gay Nineties theme of the supper club. Tonight she was wearing her emerald-green taffeta with its deep yoke of black lace, and leg of mutton sleeves. Her hair was done up in a pompadour. She tossed her velvet cape to Brian, and dropped down on the first step of the stairs.

Ben came out of the shower in a terry-cloth robe, his bare feet leaving wet tracks on the hall floor, and sat on the piano bench. Katie Rose noted the frayed shoulder seams of his old robe and thought, "I wish we weren't so *poor.*"

He and Mother exchanged fond, understanding

smiles. "So you're practically off for the auld sod?" he grinned.

"Practically in Cork County in Aunt Nellie's wee cottage with the cowshed in back," she laughed. "Katie Rose, love, unfasten these hooks and eyes in back so the stays won't be gouging me." She pulled combs and hairpins out of her hair, and ran relieved fingers through it, fluffing it into a red halo.

"Guido was sweet about my leaving," she went on. "He said for me to get off with Gran as soon as we could because you never know with an old person like Aunt Nellie—"

Jill, the blunt-spoken, said, "She might die before you get there."

Ben gave her his dark look, and Stacy swallowed a bite of ham to say, "You and your big mouth."

Mother reached into the pocket of her full skirt and triumphantly drew forth a sheaf of bills. "Guido gave me a hundred dollars vacation pay. He says he doesn't want to lose me."

She leaned against the newel post for half an hour while they talked and planned. Besides this hundred, she would have her pay before she left—

"But you'll need some yourself for the trip even with Grandda paying your fare," Ben reminded her.

"Yes, I want to bring back sweaters for you all. All the time I was playing and singing tonight, I was trying to figure whether this—plus fifty from my pay—would last for groceries for the month or five weeks I'll be gone."

"It'll be plenty," Katie Rose said. She knew heady satisfaction when Mother put the hundred dollars in her hand. And she would have fifty more. What a lot of money. Her exultation mounted when Ben said he would add an extra ten dollars a week. "I'll make good money on my construction job."

Mother expostulated that he'd need his summer pay for enrolling at the university this fall for his pre-med course. "I'll have enough," Ben insisted. "I'll give Katie Rose ten a week, and take care of the phone bill, and gas and light." But being the watchdog of the family, he added sternly, "You needn't think you can squander money, Katie Rose. Mother could never run the house on what she does if she didn't buy in quantities—"

"And if that nice Leff didn't let us have flour and all at wholesale," Mother murmured.

Katie Rose said nothing about Leff's sacks of flour that were such an eyesore. But she said firmly, "There's just one thing, Mom. If I'm to keep house and do the cooking, I want to do it my way. I mean, I don't want Stacy razzing me, and Ben bossing me and calling me the Duchess of Belford—"

Ben broke in, "Where do you get that bossing-you

stuff?" and Stacy said, "Oh but, Mom, you know what hifalutin ideas Katie Rose gets."

"It wouldn't hurt any of us to have a few more hifalutin ideas," Mother said shortly. "I always meant to have things nicer."

Katie Rose followed up her advantage. "And you know how sassy the littles—well, the twins—are. You know how they'll be when you're gone. They'll be telling me they don't have to do anything I tell them because I'm not their boss."

Mother looked around at her six children. "Katie Rose is right. It'd be a madhouse here without some-one being in charge. As long as she's willing to do all the work of buying and cooking and looking after the house, you'll have to realize she's the *mother* in my place. No talking back, no finding fault from any of you."

The littles promised they'd mind Katie Rose. Stacy held up her hand and said, "I'll be a dow-cile (she meant docile) loving sister." Ben grinned skeptically, "It'll come hard, but I won't say a word—not as long as I get enough to eat."

Katie Rose had been given the green light.

FOUR

The lull after the storm! And the Belford house this
afternoon, after Mother and Gran had set off for the
airport with Grandda, looked as though a full-sized
tornado had passed through it.

Mother wouldn't hear to the family going out to
see them off on the plane. "I can't bear helloes or good-
bys at an airport or station," she said firmly. "Gran
and I are the crying kind—"

"I'd cry too," Stacy said.

"I know." Mother's laugh was shaky. "It'd be like
a wake, and everyone would be looking around for
the coffin. I want to remember you all here in the

house and not looking woebegone at the airport."

It was a week and a day since Gran had said, "I'd like you to go with me, Rose." And a scurry-burry eight days it had been what with all the end-of-school activities, climaxed by Ben's graduation in cap and gown from John Quincy Adams the night before; with Mother's borrowing lightweight luggage, and getting her passport (complete with picture); with her taking shoulder and chest measurements of all the family for hand-knit sweaters to bring back, and then losing the paper and having to take them all over again; with her shopping for herself as well as Gran, and then trying Gran's dresses on Jill, with Jill standing ramrod stiff and disgusted, while Mother turned up the hem.

Katie Rose picked up the pair of Mother's pumps that just wouldn't crowd into her suitcase. Stacy said wanly, "You wouldn't think a house would be so empty with just—just one person gone."

A motherly voice said, "I'll make a pot of tea. There's nothing like hot tea to put heart in a body."

It was Liz, one of the Bannon relatives, who said it. She had driven in with Gran and Grandda the evening before for Ben's graduation and to stay the night. The O'Byrnes had a saying, "Never go visiting with one arm as long as the other." It meant of course never to go empty-handed. Liz hadn't. She had brought in molds of butter, blackberry jam, and two fat stewing-hens.

The rosy-faced Liz with her rich Irish brogue and motherly ways—though, as she said, she had neither chit nor child of her own—often came in and slept in the alcove off Mother's bedroom while she had her high blood pressure checked at a clinic. But from the moment Katie Rose saw the labored descent of her bulky figure from Grandda's car yesterday she had thought, "Surely Liz is just coming in for the graduation and to see the folks off. Surely she isn't planning on staying with us while Mom's away."

She was still thinking it as she watched Liz fill the big earthenware teapot with boiling water. No, surely just when Katie Rose was given full charge of the household (without benefit of a grownup) she wasn't going to have Liz here to make it difficult.

Ben gulped down his tea and went hurrying off to return his rented cap and gown. Stacy went down the block to commiserate with another summer-school student. The littles went their busy way.

Grandda returned from the airport and announced that the travelers had taken off right on the dot. He chuckled, "Poor Rose all but got cold feet at the last about leaving."

"I know," Katie Rose said as she poured his tea. "She started getting them last night."

Katie Rose had slept on the living-room couch, because of her and Stacy giving up their bed to Gran and Grandda. Mother had puttered around until late doing last-minute things. She kept drifting in to Katie Rose on the couch to air her worries. "I don't feel right about leaving Brian. He's our baby. And he takes things so to heart—he isn't like Matt or Jill—"

"I'll take care of Brian, don't you worry."

"Oh do, love, do. And Ben—did you notice how tall and thin he looked when he walked up for his diploma? Da says they'll probably put him on the cement crew —and that'll be such hard work, and he'll need a lot of food—"

"For heaven's sake, Mom, I won't starve Ben. Don't worry about him getting enough to eat."

Mother had weighed her suitcase again; that's when she took out the extra pair of pumps, and drifted back to say, "I'd hoped we could do something about that roughneck Jill this summer. Do you realize she's going on twelve? It's not natural for a girl not to like pretty dresses. Can you think of—of—well, any psychology to get her into one?"

"It'd have to be a sneak approach, or else a miracle."

Mother sighed. "Yes, a miracle, no less, to get her out of Levi's." She lit a cigarette, and added on a nervous laugh, "Gran thinks Aunt Nellie won't approve of my smoking. Do you suppose I'll have to sneak out to the cowshed everytime I want a cigarette?"

"Mom, will you get to bed? Aunt Nellie will love you. Everybody does."

Grandda said now as he stirred his tea, "Too bad the old gentleman wasn't here to see Ben graduate."

He meant their grandfather on the Belford side who lived in the old Belford home which was a landmark near the university where he had been chancellor for so many years.

"He's in Canada working on a manuscript about early poets with some old scholar he calls his confrere," Katie Rose answered absently, for Liz was getting up from the table. Surely now she'd say, "I'd better be gathering my things together so I can go back with you."

Instead she murmured, "I'll leave you two to talk. Good-by now, Urban, and I hope you won't be too lonely with your wife gone."

Sudden anger sifted through Katie Rose as she watched them shake hands. It was a frame-up. One of those hopeless conspiracies between grownups.

"Lonely, is it!" he scoffed good-naturedly, and winked at Katie Rose. "And if I am, I can always come driving down to my beautiful blackbird."

Blarney will get you no place, she thought, her fury mounting as she heard Liz's heavy tread on the stairs. She flung out, "I suppose it was your idea to drag

Liz in here to stay while Mom's in Ireland.

His heavy, tufted eyebrows lifted. "Drag Liz in? What kind of talk is that? Since when isn't she welcome?"

"How long is she going to stay?"

His look was even more reproachful. "And since when do we ask one of our own how long she'll be staying?"

But he changed the subject. "With all the to-doing over the trip to Ireland, we couldn't gather together any butter or eggs to be bringing in. Gran's little Jersey will be calving any day now, and I'll have cream piling up on me." He glanced at the sacks of flour and meal, and said, "God help us, you're almost out. But then I should be coming in about Tuesday for some special hardware. So I'll pick up an order for you at the mill. Leff will jot down the wholesale price, and you can pay me the way your mother—"

She said shortly, "No. Don't bother stopping and having Leff load you up on all those sacks of stuff."

He stared at her as though he hadn't heard right. "Sacks of stuff, is it! Wurra, blackbird, you can't run a house without flour and wheat meal for Irish bread."

"I'm not going to bake Irish bread. I'm sick of the sight of it. Nobody else has it. Everybody else buys bread that comes already sliced. We're not going to have oatmeal every morning either. Everybody else has dry breakfast food. You can get it in cartons of six so each one can have his choice."

"Phuh! It's nothing but puffed-up flavored air. Growing children and a man putting in a hard day's work need a breakfast to stick to the ribs."

She said nothing.

He took out his car keys, twirled them in puzzlement, and then went on in a more reasonable voice, "I'll be working early and late on this school job. Your gran left a little flock of fryers I'll be hard put to look after. I wonder now about bringing them in here—another week, and you can reach out for one or two for the skillet whenever you want. You aren't above dressing out a chicken, are you?"

She drew a long breath. It was now or never—her declaration of independence—her severing from old ways. She said firmly, "I'll buy chickens at the supermarket when I want them. And I'll buy butter in cubes and milk in cartons. I've got menus all planned ahead. I told Mom I'd run the house and cook the meals while she was gone, only—only I want to do it *my* way."

His smoldering blue eyes under knitted brows stared at her. "Do you mean to sit there and tell me you want none of the hams and bacons and chunks of fresh meat I keep in my freezer locker for you? And none of my rich Jersey cream?"

She repeated, "I'll buy what I need from the supermarket."

Grandda had the quick flaring temper that went with his red hair. He stood up and whammed his car keys hard against the dinette table. "Well of all the hoity-toity little pieces! Then do it your way, my fine miss. But if you get yourself out on a limb, don't think you can come yelping to me for help. Hell'll freeze over before I bring you in so much as a banty egg."

And though Katie Rose's hair was smoky black, that same O'Byrne temper had been passed on to her. She flung back, "You needn't worry. You'd be the last one I'd go yelping to for help."

He banged the back door as he went out. She heard the angry sputter of his car as it left the curb and went roaring down Hubbell Street.

Her hands were shaking. Oh dear, they shouldn't have parted like that. She had meant to be tactful in refusing all those Bannon donations. ("They're not *donations,*" Ben had once corrected her. "Our house is their headquarters when they come to Denver. They wouldn't feel right if they didn't bring things.")

Yes, she had meant to explain to Grandda that in cooking school all the recipes called for cubes of butter, not the kind you scooped out of bowls. And that the thick cream that came from Bannon in Mason jars was so rich it made drop cookies run all over the pan.

But she had let her anger at Liz's staying get the best of her.

It was the first time Grandda had ever left without kissing her and singing out, "Bye, Bye, Blackbird."

And she still had a session with Liz to go through. For Liz too must be made to realize that the old order had changed.

Katie Rose sat there and took stock. She wouldn't start her regime today when everyone felt wilted and empty. And maybe not tomorrow. Liz would be putting on her two hens to stew. Well, let her. Let her bake her Irish bread.

Tomorrow morning Katie Rose and Jeanie were going to that new shopping center with Miguel. While he was outside the store taking pictures of shoppers, she could do her shopping. Jeanie had only to buy cans of fruit juice for punch which they were to take to a shower in the afternoon.

It was to be a surprise shower for Beany Buell's new little son. Beany Buell, nee Malone, and her husband, Carl, lived next door to the Kincaids in Harmony Heights. Beany had taught a club of girls at a community center, and the club was giving the shower for her six-weeks-old boy who had been christened James William.

Jeanie, her brown eyes dancing, had told Katie Rose how Carl would bring all the girls over from the center; they, in turn, would bring refreshments. "But I told him you and I would make the punch because that'll give us a chance to crash the party. Won't it be fun?"

Katie Rose thought on. Come to think of it, she had better wait until Monday to launch her new program of tea in the living room, and dinner (not supper) in the dining room. For Sundays were always disorganized days with everyone coming and going. But Monday morning Ben would leave early for his new job, and Stacy would leave a little later for summer school.

She needn't have dreaded her session with Liz. She came into the kitchen and helped clear the tea things away. Katie Rose announced, "I'm going to run the house *different* from the way Mom did. I'm going to cook *different*."

Liz said blandly, "Are you now? That'll be nice, childeen. We old folks can get in a rut. It's good to try new ways."

She took from the pocket of her shapeless wool skirt a ten-dollar bill and laid it on the table. "Here, dear one, that'll be by way of helping with the groceries. I've some fillings to be seeing a dentist about, and then this blood pressure. And while I'm here I've in mind finding a new afghan pattern, and knitting one for a wedding present."

"But, Liz, you mustn't *pay*. You're one of our own. Why, Mother would die if she thought—"

"Never mind, never mind now. This is just between us. And it's little enough, dear knows, to be paying each week I'm here."

Another ten added to Ben's, and added to the backlog Mother had left! Katie Rose couldn't wait till tomorrow morning and her trip to the new Maplewood Mart with Miguel.

FIVE

Jeanie Kincaid was with Miguel when he came the next morning to take Katie Rose to the Grand Opening of the new supermarket out on the edge of town.

His camera was strapped over his shoulder, and he said, "I'm driving Gramp's Dodge this morning. I don't mind squashing you gals down in the Triumph, but not my camera. Not when I have to take pictures of satisfied customers coming out of the Maplewood Mart. The littles told me Liz was here." He raised his voice and shouted through the house, "Liz, acushla, where are you?"

She came down the stairs, and enfolded Miguel's

lanky figure to her ample bosom. "Ah, boyeen—my own boyeen," she said fondly.

Some ten years ago when Liz lived in Ireland, she had boarded Miguel and his father while Michael Parnell, the writer, gathered material for his book on Ireland.

"I saw the six-page ad Maplewood Mart ran in the morning paper," Katie Rose said. "I'm taking my shopping list along." She was also taking two of the twenty-dollar bills her mother left.

"They're giving carnations to all the women customers and balloons to the children," Liz said. "They even have specials on paperback books."

"Come along with us, Liz," Miguel said, and Liz with her love of fanfare and people needed little urging.

He helped her into the front seat. "My best girl gets to ride up here with me. But you, Petunia, get to hold the camera on your lap."

He took the long drive east and north. Liz wanted to know all about his father. Miguel told her he had finished the Alaska book and was now in Washington, D.C., checking all his historical data at the Congressional Library.

"Might be I'd drive out there too. Pop always counts on my reading his books before he winds them up—he wants to get the reaction of the stupid reader,

I guess. Especially on what he calls 'human interest.' "

"You're not the stupid reader," Liz contradicted loyally.

At the active new shopping center Miguel parked in the crowded parking lot. His co-worker showed him where to take up a strategic position outside the store with his camera. Katie Rose, Jeanie, and Liz went through the open door into the brightly lighted maelstrom. Music was playing. Carnations were pinned on their shoulders by young girls in drum majorette costumes. They were given numbers for a drawing on a color TV, and a paper cup of Hawaiian fruit juice.

Liz found that she had forgotten her glasses, and Jeanie said, "I'll help her pick out her whodunits, because it won't take me long to buy the fruit juice for Beany's shower. You go ahead with your shopping, Katie Rose."

Katie Rose pushed her basket on wheels through the store in pure ecstasy. A dream come true. She loaded in butter in wrapped cubes, and uncracked eggs in cartons. Flat packages of sliced bacon, cellophane-wrapped ham slices. Sandwich meats and spreads for the lunches Ben would be taking. Pork chops to be baked with dressing (packaged) *à la* Mrs. McHarg. At the frozen food counter she picked out vegetables, french fries, deveined shrimp, and spinach soufflé.

She piled in cake and muffin mixes and packaged icings, and six-pack cartons of breakfast food. Canned mushrooms, consommé, chicken. And here were the slivered almonds that would turn her frozen green beans into beans almondine.

Oh, the joy of halting at the dairy counter, and reaching for slice'n bake cookies, canned biscuits, cheese cakes, brown'n serve rolls! She found a special on frozen waffles—eight packages for a dollar. She had eaten these hot from the toaster at the McHargs'.

Bread. She might as well buy for a week while she was here. She bought an assortment of fruit for the sideboard, also *à la* McHarg.

Life's niceties certainly came a little higher than she expected. When she checked out, the cashier gave her back only thirty-seven cents from her forty dollars.

Katie Rose pushed her sacked purchases in the wire basket out the door and to the spot where they had left Miguel. Jeanie and Liz were already waiting there. Jeanie held a sack of fruit juices, and Liz her four or five paperbacks.

Miguel said, "You timed it about right, Petunia. I think one more picture will finish me up. The management told us to snap just one shopper—not a bunch together, because they don't want to hand out five dollars' worth of credit *en masse*. Let's see if I can catch one lone man or woman."

Katie Rose halted her loaded basket. Standing beside Miguel, they all looked through the outpouring of shoppers. Their eyes passed over a family group of man, wife, and two children with balloons. A bevy of teenagers followed, giggling because they had somehow accrued more than one carnation apiece.

Jeanie, interested in picture-taking, moved closer to Miguel and peered through the finder of the camera. She said, "Let me sight somone for you, and I'll tell you when to click it."

Again it was the garish, oversize flowers in the dress that drew Katie Rose's attention to the wearer. Would you believe it! There was the same blond hair, looking even more bleached and dead in the bright sunlight. Katie Rose nudged Jeanie, "For gosh sakes!—there's the dog-burger woman we saw at Wetzel's that day. See, just behind that man carrying a little boy on his shoulder."

Jeanie looked up from the camera. Again her face puckered into a puzzled frown. "You'd think she'd sew up that ripped hem," she muttered.

Miguel too glanced at the woman. She was alone. One hand held a sack from which green onion tops protruded; the other carried a rectangular box of pansies in full bloom. She came toward them with her preening, hippy walk.

Miguel said, "We'll catch her, Jeanie."

Just at that moment the woman saw Jeanie standing beside Miguel who was aiming his camera at her. She stopped so short that her sack tilted far over to the side. For a brief moment she stared at them aghast, her face slack in amazement—or was it terror?

"Just hold it till—"

Miguel never finished the sentence. The woman screamed out a profane epithet, and hurled the box of pansies. It hit the camera with such force that the thin wooden slats that held the box together broke open. Pansies and black loam were spewed over the two behind the camera and on the ground at their feet.

Without stopping to pick up the onions and grapefruit that spilled from her sack the woman turned and ran like someone pursued, into the maze of parked cars.

Miguel and Jeanie, Liz and Katie Rose could only stand in stunned surprise at the unexpected attack. A passing shopper muttered, "Well I'll be darned!" Another said, "That's a good way to wreck a camera."

His remark seemed to rouse the dazed Miguel. "Hey, Petunia, run and get her license number, and if she's wrecked Pop's camera—"

She ran in the direction the woman had taken. But it was like trying to find the proverbial needle in a haystack. So many cars were pulling in or going out. She had to step out of the way of a truck that was backing up, and dodge a convertible that came swooping in. She had just time to glimpse a faded chocolate brown and pink car as it hurtled out of a far exit.

She went back to the scene of confusion. Miguel was blowing the dirt off his camera. Jeanie, head bent, flicked her fingers through her thick brown hair. Katie Rose panted out, "She got away before I could see her license number."

By now the dropped grapefruit had been kicked out of sight and the bunch of green onions mashed flat by passing feet. Liz was trying to salvage the shambles that had been made of the box of pansies. She scooped up some of the dirt and put it back in the broken box, and gathered up wisps of pansy plants.

"Oh, for heaven's sake, Liz!" Katie Rose scolded.

"I hate to see the poor flowers trampled on."

Miguel's partner in the picture-taking project had joined him. "It doesn't matter about the picture. Between us, we've got more than enough to sort through and pick out the best. But I hope your camera isn't damaged."

"Lordy, I hope not," Miguel muttered.

At last, groceries and passengers were loaded into Miguel's car. He maneuvered it out of its crowded space and drove home.

Jeanie unpinned the red carnation on her shoulder. She tried shaking the dirt out of it, but the wet black soil had already smudged it. She threw it away, and said in a strained voice, "She looked up and recognized me. She threw the box of pansies at *me*."

"She threw it at the camera," Miguel said. "But I can't figure why she'd go berserk at the sight of one."

Liz, in the front seat, was trying to work a broken slat of the pansy box under the wire that held them all in place. "She was scared out of her wits. Even so, I'd like to get my hands on her—the vixen. Banging flowers around like that."

The long drive out to Maplewood Mart, the shopping, and the drive back had taken the morning. It was well past noon when Miguel, after dropping Jeanie off, helped carry in the Belford groceries. No, he told Liz, he couldn't stop for lunch. He was to meet his fellow photographer at his shop to develop their pictures.

Katie Rose deposited all her beautiful purchases in the refrigerator and cupboards. She arranged and re arranged them. She surveyed them, and gloated over them. She found a silver bowl in which to pile her fruit arrangement. She was out gathering grape leaves to line the bowl when Liz called her to the telephone.

It was Jeanie. "Can you come early and give me a hand at making the punch? Mom is substituting at Mount Carmel, and I don't know when she'll be back.

I just *have* to wash my hair. I thought I could brush that smelly dirt out of it but—"

"Wash your hair! Why, Jeanie, it's past two and the shower for Beany is at three."

"I can use the dryer while we're stirring up the brew."

Katie Rose lost no time in taking a shower and putting on her coral-colored summer dress. (A girl could always dress quicker for a party where no boys were present.) Ben had taken the car to buy heavy work-clothes for his job, which meant that Katie Rose must walk the ten or twelve blocks from Hubbell Street to the Kincaid home in Harmony Heights.

She took all the short cuts. The pink door of the low white ranch house was open, and Jeanie called out, "Come on in. I'm here in the kitchen."

Katie Rose halted in the kitchen doorway in surprise. No electric dryer encased Jeanie's wet head. "Your hair is sopping," Katie Rose exclaimed.

"Yes—wouldn't you know?—the electric cord went haywire on the dryer." She opened the refrigerator door, and stood irresolute as though her thoughts were far away. "I can't seem to remember what you said you mixed with what when you made the punch for the fashion-show reception."

Katie Rose dropped her sweater on a high stool, and reached for frosted cans from the icebox. "Pineapple and grapefruit juice for the base. And raspberry to color it, and lemon juice to keep it from being too sweetish." She glanced at the limp wet towel Jeanie held, and added, "Get a dry towel and rub your hair."

Jeanie disregarded that. She ran a small can through the wall can opener. "Katie Rose, when that bleached dog-burger woman bent over at Wetzel's and the roots of her hair showed so plain—remember? What shade would you say her hair really was?"

"Sort of a cinnamon-brown—something like yours, only maybe darker. What in the world are you asking that for?"

Absently Jeanie deposited the open can on the work-table. She set it so close to the edge that it toppled over, spilling frozen slush onto the floor. She reached for a mop to wipe it up. "This just isn't my day." She bent her head and asked, "Can you still smell that *manury* smell of the black dirt in my hair? I had the darndest time getting it out."

Katie Rose sniffed hastily, "Smells just like shampoo. Look at the time, Jeanie. Shall I get out the ice cubes?"

They were working busily when Jeanie's mother came in with a paper sack and hurried apologies, "I didn't mean to be so late. Oh, you're helping, Katie Rose. I bought more lemons in case you need them. We mustn't forget the punch bowl and glasses." And then, "Jeanie! Whatever possessed you to wash your hair just before Beany's party?"

Both girls explained about the woman aiming her box of pansies at the camera and the spattering of black dirt, as well as about the electric dryer which wasn't functioning.

Mrs. Kincaid promptly armed herself with a heavy towel and began drying Jeanie's hair, explaining ruefully to Katie Rose, "I guess her dad and I are overly cautious about Jeanie and wet hair. But the worst cold and infection in her ear came on the day she was six. Remember, Jeanie, how I washed your hair that morning for your birthday party, and then you got so sick we had to call it off?"

"It wasn't my wet hair. It was a bug—you came down with it too, remember?"

"Indeed I do."

Jeanie peered out from under the towel to ask suddenly, "Mom, that day my mother left me at Mount Carmel, did you *see* her?"

Her mother's face turned blank with surprise. "Why, child, what makes you ask? I mean—now—"

"Just curiosity, I guess. Did you *see* her?"

"No—that is, if I did I didn't remember—"

"Didn't anybody see her that remembers? I don't see how anybody could leave a baby at a nursery without *somebody* seeing her."

Her mother said with a flustered laugh, "Look at the time—it's almost three. And Carl Buell said he'd bring all the girls from Beany's community center at three. Aren't you going to change your dress?"

Jeanie was still wearing the brown sleeveless linen she had worn to Maplewood Mart. "This'll do," she said briefly. "You've never told me anything about it, except that I was left at Mount Carmel."

Her mother fingered the towel with nervous fingers, but she said gently, "That's about all there is to tell, honey. It was on a Saturday—and on Saturdays we held the baby clinic at the nursery. That was the morning for polio shots, and there was a regular flock of mothers with children. We were never so rushed. I had to help the nurse, and your father was giving shots, and some of the youngsters were screaming their lungs out—"

She paused for breath, and went on, "And then when things began to calm down a bit, we noticed a blanketed baby on a chair that didn't seem to belong to anyone. I asked questions, and a Mexican woman— we had a time getting it out of her because she didn't speak English—said a young woman had left it there. I vaguely remembered seeing a girl come in with a baby in her arms. And only a vague remembrance that she had a scarf tied over her head—but nearly everyone did because it was a drizzly morning."

"Can't you even remember whether she was tall or short?"

Katie Rose was stirring the red raspberry juice into the pale liquid in the pitcher. She gave a start at the insistence in Jeanie's voice. But surely—oh, surely, her question had nothing to do with the woman in the flowered dress with the wide hem so noticeably turned up! Yet Katie Rose slowed her stirring, somehow hoping Mrs. Kincaid would answer, "No, she was tall—about the same height I am."

Instead she shook her head. "I just don't know, sweet. So many women came in carrying babies that morning with scarfs over their heads."

"Didn't she say anything to the Mexican woman even? Or leave a note like they do in stories?"

"Yes, she left a note tucked inside the blanket. It said—I still know the words by heart, 'My baby is sick and I can't take care of her. Please take good care of her. She was born April 1.'"

"*Was* the baby sick?" Katie Rose asked curiously.

"Yes—a cold that could go into pneumonia. The doctor and I worked with her all day. We took her home—we lived on Downing Street then—and we both worked with her all night. And by morning she was better and we—" her voice thickened. She turned to Jeanie and changed the "she" to "you." "And we had a feeling you were *ours*—and that life wouldn't be worth living without you." She added on a shaky smile, "That was our and your first introduction to a vapor kettle. We turned our copper teapot into one."

Jeanie's own eyes were moist. "I remember that old copper teapot. That was the one the nurse let boil dry, and the spout dropped off."

"That wasn't the only thing that miserable nurse did," Mrs. Kincaid grunted.

With that came the sound of cars stopping in the driveway of the Buell house next door. And the slam of car doors, accompanied by a glad shrieking of girlish voices, "Surprise, Miss Beany! Surprise—Surprise!"

Katie Rose and Jeanie crowded to the window to see the disgorging of girls from Carlton's station wagon, and more from a pickup truck. Jeanie said, "Carlton told us that a friend of Beany's named Dulcie might have to bring the overflow. I'm anxious to meet Dulcie. Remember, Mom, how Beany laughs so about Dulcie always telling her exactly how to take care of the baby?"

"Yes, and how to run her life." Mrs. Kincaid laughed as though she were relieved to have a different topic of conversation. "It seems that Dulcie married before Beany, and had a baby before she did. And Dulcie likes to crow over Beany because she's got a houseful of furniture and Beany hasn't. These girls that got up the shower call themselves the Ho-Ho's—it's short for Homemaking and Hobby Club. They all call Beany 'Miss Beany' and Carlton 'Mr. Bull' instead of 'Mr. Buell.' "

"Beany's husband isn't staying for the party," Katie Rose said as the station wagon backed out of the driveway.

"No, he said he'd dump off the girls and then go on to the baseball game his community center team is playing." Jeanie ran a comb through her ruffled-up hair and said gaily, "We're off. Katie Rose, if you can juggle the punch bowl and cups, I'll take the pitcher of juice. Here, hook some cups over my fingers."

Mrs. Kincaid held the door open for them. Jeanie stopped outside the door. "Just one more question, Mom. Did you keep the note that was tucked under my blanket?"

Again surprise blanked out her mother's smile. "No—no. We destroyed it when your life began with us. Well—after we went through legal channels and adopted you."

Jeanie bent over the huge glass bowl and kissed her. "That was my lucky day," she said.

"Ours too," her mother said. "Ours too, darling."

SIX

Beany Buell greeted the new arrivals at the door, her face all flushed excitement under its sprinkling of freckles. "So you two were in on it too? This is one surprise party that was a surprise."

The Buell house was laid out on the same plan as the Kincaid house next door. But the rooms were smaller, and noticeably lacking in furniture and carpeting.

A pert, pretty, and bustling young woman reached for their contributions. "I'm Dulcie," she announced. "I'll thin the punch down with water. Though I don't know what we can set the bowl and glasses on. Beany, *when* are you and Carl going to get some dining-room furniture?"

Beany winked at Katie Rose and Jeanie. *"When* Carl doesn't have to pay tuition at law school."

She introduced Katie Rose and Jeanie to the dozen or so members of the Ho-Ho Club. There were Italian and Mexican girls, one Negro girl, two blond girls who giggled over everything or nothing, and a doll-like Japanese who had brought the cake with its ornate icing of pink rosebuds and blue forget-me-nots.

One wispy little girl named Violetta, who was younger than the others, took it upon herself to pass out information to Katie Rose and Jeanie. She indicated the shy and demure Japanese girl, "She brought the cake because her father is a cake-icer. For Fourth of July he makes red, white, and blue flags on cakes."

Violetta nodded toward the baby, perhaps nine or ten months old, sitting upright on the floor clutching a miniature car. "That's Dulcie's. Dulcie puts ruffles on everything so people will know she's a girl."

Dulcie, hearing that, admitted with disarming frankness, "Isn't it awful? Here, I always wanted a pretty girl I could make fluffy-ruffle clothes for. And look at her! Sober and rawboned—just like her dad."

The little girl had certainly not inherited her mother's rose-petal skin or sparkling blue eyes. Her skin was sallow and her eyes grave and unblinking.

Dulcie's thick hair, the color of burnt sugar, was worn in a pony tail that cascaded down her back like a wavy plume. The baby's hair was scant and straight and clung tight to her scalp. She looked like a miniature man dressed in a ruffled sunsuit.

"She'd rather play with a hammer and nails than a doll," Dulcie lamented.

The center of the gay celebration was the very small, very pink-faced James William Buell who was yawning prodigiously when Beany carried him out of the bedroom. The Ho-Ho's gift to him was a bassinet which Katie Rose could see had already seen much service. But the girls had repainted it white and trimmed it lavishly with blue taffeta. James William was deposited in it.

The know-it-all Violetta informed Katie Rose and Jeanie, "The reason they put that great big bow on the end is to cover up where a hole is big as a saucer."

One of the older girls added, "It was my Geraldine who kicked the hole in it."

"Oh! Are you married?" Katie Rose asked.

"I was," came the answer. "I'm living with my parents now."

Katie Rose and Jeanie exchanged looks. That was the nice thing about going places together; they could always share their my-goodness thoughts.

By now the Ho-Ho girls had happily deposited

themselves on the floor. Dulcie remarked loudly, "At our house we've got enough chairs to seat fifteen easy."

Violetta, whose black adoring eyes followed her hostess's every move, defended her. "But Miss Beany and Mr. Buell have got that love seat and it's a hundred years old—or maybe older." (Katie Rose and Jeanie had the honor of sitting on it.)

Dulcie got in the last word, "I don't like old stuff."

The gay and happy afternoon wore on. The cake, as pleasing to the palate as to the eye, was demolished except for a sizeable slice left for "Mr. Bull." The pink punch was a big success.

When the small inmate in the blue-trimmed bassinet began to complain hungrily, Katie Rose and Jeanie stood up. They said their good-bys and left.

Outside the sky was clouded over and the air had turned chill. Katie Rose wriggled into her sweater. It was always customary when the girls visited each other for one to walk a "piece" with the departing one. But this late afternoon when Jeanie's mother was working on a rose trellis in front of the house, she called across to ask, "Is it all right if I walk all the way home with Katie Rose?"

Her mother called back, "Wait a minute." She hurried into the house and came back with a fluffy white sweater. She held it for Jeanie and even pulled it close together in front. "I'm one of these awful coddly mothers," she said with an apologetic laugh to the two girls.

They walked toward Hubbell Street with Katie Rose chattering about the party they had left, and Jeanie making only monosyllabic answers. They had gone only a few blocks when they saw Liz, well laden with bundles, also on her way to Hubbell Street.

The girls stopped to wait for her. They relieved her of her packages and stood for a minute while she caught her breath. She had been to the University Hills shopping center to buy yarn and a new pattern for an afghan. "I'm always long on plans but short on breath," Liz said as they walked on.

As they passed Wetzel's store Jeanie looked at it and, as though it evoked a disturbing memory, suddenly flung out, "I wish I'd never laid eyes on that dog-burger, pansy-throwing woman. Remember, Liz, we told you about seeing her there and how Mr. Wetzel mentioned that Dr. Kincaid might be stopping for cheese? And you remember, Katie Rose, how she couldn't get out of the store fast enough?"

"You said she must owe your dad a doctor bill and that's why she went tearing off without so much as a by-your-leave."

"And then this morning she looked up and recognized me, and wham!—a box of pansies came my way."

"Came the camera's way," corrected Liz. "She was scared out of her boots of having her picture taken."

"Out of her runover sandals," put in Katie Rose.

Jeanie walked on with them, squinching her nose as she always did when she was puzzled.

Katie Rose felt her troubled uneasiness. Always before it had been Katie Rose who, when life was upsetting or bruising, had reached out to Jeanie's warm understanding and help. Now the roles were reversed. And Katie Rose felt helpless as to what to say that would comfort her.

They reached the corner house on Hubbell and were as joyfully welcomed by Cully as though they had been away for weeks instead of hours. They fought him off and went through the back door and dropped Liz's purchases on the dinette table. Liz said, "Mavourneen, slide the teakettle on. Isn't it awful, Jeanie, the way we always head for the kitchen like cattle for the feed trough?"

Jeanie didn't smile back. She only stood huddled into her sweater as though she were chilled and lost.

Liz said gently, "You mustn't let that flighty fool of a woman trouble you, little one."

Jeanie's words fairly tumbled out, "Mom was telling us before we went to Beany's party about the rainy Saturday morning when I was left on a chair at Mount Carmel. But I just wish somebody knew whether the

girl or woman that left me was tall—or short like I
am. I wish I knew whether Mom was telling the truth
or not. I wish—I just wish that woman didn't have
hair sort of the color of mine—"

Katie Rose halted in her pouring of boiling water
into the teapot. "Jeanie! What in the world are you
thinking?"

"I don't know," she said shakily. "I only know
what I can't help thinking—and that's that Dad knew
my mother. I think she must have been one of his
patients and was a neglectful, no-good person—maybe
a drunk. And that's why he's so strict and watchful,
because he's afraid I'll be like her."

"Hush, child, hush!" Liz scolded. "How can you
mistake loving concern for mistrust? You're letting
your foolish imagination run away with you. Just because that empty-headed vixen happened to cross your
path—"

"But I keep remembering the way she looked at me
at Wetzel's and the awful look on her face this morning—"

"Remember instead the things you should remember—the love of your father and mother," Liz interrupted earnestly. "Forget these other happenstances.
Ah, I've often found a good forgetter more helpful
than a good memory for darksome, worrisome things."

Jeanie's face lightened. "You're wonderful, Liz—

you're a blessing to mankind. As of right now, I'm cultivating a good forgetter."

"Now we'll all have a cuppa tea," Liz said. She was convinced that steaming hot tea was the cure-all for every ill.

They were gathered at the dinette table with full cups before them when the slam of a car door was followed by Cully's hysterical yelps. And very shortly an exuberant Ben pushed through the door, his arms piled high with khaki clothes, and a huge shoe box riding on top of them and held in place by his chin.

"All I had to buy was work boots," he told them. He had stopped at the bakery on the Boulevard where one of Mother's good friends worked. "Pearl had a brother that just finished his stint in the army, and he left all these shirts and pants with her. So she gave them to me—said she was glad to get rid of them."

"Do they fit you?" Katie Rose asked.

"Good enough. The guy was evidently a little bigger in the chest, and not so long in the legs, but for muckin' cement that won't matter. Look, Jeanie, as long as I saved so much dough on my workclothes, how about us celebrating? I ran into a couple of graduates from Adams, and they tell me there's to be a big whoop-te-do out at the Red Barn tonight. You know that new place where they dance square dances and polkas? Be fun, won't it?"

Jeanie said on a sigh, "I'd love to. Only you know the old third degree you'll have to go through with Dad. He'll have to know whether you'll be driving, and what time we'll be back, and who runs the place, and do they serve beer."

There was no dampening Ben. "It's worth it to have a date with you." He chuckled. "I won't let on that I'm taking you out to get you soused."

"Such talk!" Liz reproved. "You ought to be ashamed."

Jeanie giggled gleefully.

SEVEN

Life took another unexpected turn for Katie Rose. The next evening, Sunday, Miguel phoned her. He was calling from the airport. He told her of his father telephoning him that morning from Washington to say he had found an apartment not far from the Congressional Library. And he wanted Miguel to join him there.

"I thought I could drive out, but he said no, I'd better fly. And you know how fast that guy works. He checked the airlines and found out there was a seat on this plane that's leaving at five-forty. Yipes, it kept me jumping to get packed. The fellow across the alley drove me out. They're calling my plane now. But look, Petunia, I want you to keep the TR for me. Gramps said he didn't want that kiddie-car left on his hands. There isn't room in the garage for it, and I can't leave it sitting out in front."

"What? You want me to keep the Triumph for you?"

"I left the keys in it, and you go get it. It's yours to have and to hold and drive till I get back."

"Why, Miguel!" she gasped. "Oh my goodness, I can't think of anything so wonderful."

"That's because you're a wonderful girl. I'll feel better with you looking after it."

"I will, Miguel. I'll take good care of it. I've been worrying about how I was going to get to the supermarket when Ben will be driving our car to work every day. I can't believe it. How long will you be gone?"

"I don't know, Petunia Rose. Depends on how long it takes Pop to get his Alaska book in shape. But I'll write you and send you my address—and you write me."

"You bet I will. Miguel, we'll miss you—"

"Same here." He was talking faster now. "Any time Liz needs to go any place, you take her in the TR. I'd like to think of you and my nice little bug together. I've got to rush for Gate 9 now. Bye, honey bunch."

The receiver went up on her heartfelt, "Miguel, I

can't thank you enough—I'm so happy," and his, "Be happy till I get back."

A blue Triumph with bucket seats and white sidewalls to have and to hold and to drive until Miguel returned! Blessed Miguel! Blessed life! She couldn't wait to get her hands on the wheel.

Ben walked with her to Miguel's grandparents' where the small blue car sat in front of the house. Before she could drive off, they both had to listen to the old gentleman's irate comments on sports cars. You had to sit in one doubled up like a jackknife. Roller skates! They were a menace on the road.

Katie Rose slowed at the first corner. Feeling overweening pride in her new possession, she said, "Let's go to Jeanie's."

Dr. Kincaid opened the door and ushered them in. Jeanie came out of her room when she heard their voices. Her mother brought in Cokes.

But there was an atmosphere of tension in the living room Katie Rose had never felt in the house before. She felt it all the time she told of Miguel's sudden trip to Washington and his leaving his small car for her; all the time the doctor and Ben talked about his new road-building job, and his entering the university this fall.

The silences that fell were such *loud* silences. To fill a lull, Katie Rose said, "Tomorrow, I'm starting my new and different regime at the Belford homestead."

Jeanie gave an unmirthful laugh. "Lucky you! I'd like something new and different. I had a chance to work three evenings a week behind the refreshment counter at the Pant." (The Pant was short for the Pantages movie house on the Boulevard.) "I'd have loved selling popcorn and candy bars and seeing all the people. But Dad turned thumbs down on it."

Dr. Kincaid was a big man with craggy, resolute features, and Katie Rose thought fleetingly: If I were sick, I'd like him to come in the door.

He said reasonably, "But, Jeanie, you'd be working till about midnight. There'd always be the problem of your getting home safely."

Jeanie's eyes flicked toward Katie Rose. "See what I mean?" they fairly said. She turned to Ben and said, "I thought maybe you'd offer to bring me home."

Ben looked nonplussed. "I would any night I could," he said slowly. "You know that. But when I talked to the boss about my job, he said that if he got in a bind to finish a road contract I might be working the night shift."

Jeanie shrugged and said blithely, "So I'm to spend three days a week at the clinic where Dad can keep an eye on me. It's such thrilling work—addressing envelopes and sending duns to all the deadbeats."

Another silence. Ben filled it by imitating Miguel's

grandfather, and his sputtery wrath at what he called "roller skates."

Katie Rose and Ben didn't stay long.

The new and different regime, with Katie Rose in command, got off to a flying start on Monday. Before she even put on the coffee, she carried the offending sacks of flour and meal down to the basement and thrust them in a corner. She pulled the bamboo curtain to shut off the dinette from the kitchen.

On the breakfast table she set out the small individual cartons of breakfast food. She toasted those neat and beautiful slices of baker's bread.

A pound of bacon, a dozen eggs went like chaff in the wind. Of course, at the McHargs' one egg constituted a serving. Not at the Belfords'. Grandda O'Byrne had even remarked once that it didn't seem worthwhile dirtying a fork for one egg.

Ben, swinging his lunch bucket, departed at seven-thirty. Eight to four-thirty were his new hours. At eight, Stacy set off for her morning of make-up lit and Latin at summer school. Liz decided to go downtown and poke around.

Alone in the house—for the littles were not the kind to be underfoot when they might be asked to help—Katie Rose swept, scrubbed, and burnished the house. It was certainly disheartening to see how her fruit centerpiece on the sideboard had dwindled. Those lit-tles! No doubt every time they passed by, they snatched at the grapes and peaches and plums. Yet it would spoil the whole effect to put up a sign, "Not for eating. For looking at."

She hunted for candlesticks on the top shelf of the cupboard. The ones she found were not to her liking; they were tall, and the ones in which candles flickered on the McHarg table were squat. But while rummag-ing through that top shelf, she struck pay dirt: Mother's seldom-used tea set that had been a wedding present, complete with sugar, creamer, and even sugar tongs for lifting cubes of sugar.

She was polishing the set when Stacy returned from school, and when the clunk of bicycles against the porch announced that hunger had brought the littles home.

"I didn't realize it was noon already," Katie Rose said.

"You go ahead. I'll fix cocoa and sandwiches for us. Hm-mm, the whole house looks shiny and elegant. The question is, how long will it stay this way?"

"It's got to stay this way," Katie Rose said grimly.

"Look, Sis, you've always wanted a room of your own. How about my moving into Mom's room with Liz while Mom's in Ireland? I'm still buttering you up on account of that cream-colored creation of yours with the purple belt—*and* pumps—*and* necklace."

"Oh, Stacy, would you move in with Liz?" How Katie Rose would relish having a room without slap-happy Stacy strewing curlers and candy-bar papers about, without her spilling bath powder over the vanity, and leaving washed damp sweaters on the bed. The privacy that Katie Rose craved was hard come by in such a big family.

She went outside to get flowers for the table. There was little to choose from. The lilac bush by the ashpit was not in full bloom yet, while apple blossoms had already sifted to the ground.

But their neighbor across the fence offered her some of her irises. The neighbor was the talkative type. In return for yellow and purple irises, Katie Rose had to answer questions about her mother's leaving—and no, she didn't know how long she'd be gone.

She was edging toward the house and saying, "Oh, we'll get along fine. I'm running the house," when the littles banged out the kitchen door and made for their bikes. They were eating sandwiches and stuffing a few extras, along with baseball mitts and a bat, in their canvas paper bags while Cully circled devotedly and hopefully about. Brian gave him part of his sandwich.

Katie Rose called after them, "We'll have tea at five."

Inside the house, Stacy was calling from the top of the stairs that she was wearing her, Katie Rose's, swimsuit. "You know the one you had at Adams High." She came pelting down the stairs for Katie Rose to fasten the back zipper of her green cotton dress over it. "Not that this suit of yours is what you'd call sexsational but—"

"Stacy! *Sen*sational."

"But as soon as I get enough baby-sitting money, I'm going to splurge on a white satin one and a cap all covered with flower petals—rubber. And when I do you can borrow them."

"Where are you going swimming? And who with?"

"Bruce will be by any minute to pick me up. He's lifeguarding part-time at Coral Sands. Imagine!—he's trying to interest me in water-skiing."

Katie Rose felt only a brief twinge at hearing that name. Bruce Scerie was one of her schoolmates. She had gone through wistful, wishing months of wanting to be Bruce's girl. It had been a rocking jolt when Bruce showed preference for her bouncy and younger red-headed sister.

But Miguel had thought enough of Katie Rose to leave his TR with her. And besides, that older and wiser young man, Perry McHarg, had asked her to lunch at the Golden Slipper. He must have been more interested than she thought. And besides, she was now a dedicated housewife.

A cream-colored convertible stopped in front with a handsome dark-haired athlete at the wheel. (He looks so immature, Katie Rose told herself.) She called after Stacy, too, to be home for tea at five.

She wanted the whole family to see how tea *should* be served.

Up until now, it had always been a snatch-as-snatch-can affair. "Just something to stay you till supper," Mother always said, as she made strong tea in the big earthenware pot, and put on the dinette table a pitcher of milk to cool and weaken it. The loaf of Irish bread sat on the table, along with a bowl of untidy butter, and a jar of blackberry jam to dip into.

But Katie Rose would pattern her tea after the ones she had been served when she called on Grandfather Belford and her aunt in the Belford mansion. Silver tea service in the living room. Lemon slices stuck with cloves. Dainty rolled or open-face sandwiches. And *petits fours*. She'd had to compromise on those. She had found none at the Maplewood Mart, so had bought small assorted cookies instead.

Her timing was right. Ben dragged in after four-thirty, his face scarlet, and his new boots spattered with cement. "Just give me a few minutes in the shower," he said.

Liz drifted in from shopping or perhaps a visit at the clinic. Liz, being the visity kind, always made friends with the clerks in stores, the patients who waited with her in a doctor's or dentist's office.

Stacy came bursting in, her red hair still wet and her cheeks flushed from sun and water. She looked at the dinette table. "Where's the tea? I'm hungry as a werewolf."

"We're having it in the living room."

"Oh la-de-da!" But remembering her promise to Mother not to criticize, she clamped her hand to her mouth.

"Tea in the living room!" Jill repeated. "I didn't know we had company."

"Other people *always* serve tea in the living room."

It had taken her over an hour to trim the crusts from bread slices, to cream the butter and mix in chopped parsley and seasonings for her small rolled sandwiches. They were gone in five minutes.

All the young Belfords reached for the milk instead of the clove-stuck lemon slices. All but Katie Rose, who commented, "We are the only ones I know who put milk in tea."

"Is that so?" Liz marveled. She hesitated, and then she too dropped a lemon slice in her tea. "They look so pretty, Katie Rose."

Another five minutes, and the second pot of tea

was empty and so was the plate of assorted cookies. Ben swung his long legs onto the couch, his bare feet prodding Jill off her end of it. He stretched out, smiled wearily at them all and muttered, "I don't think I could even make the stairs," and promptly fell asleep.

When Katie Rose cleared away the tea things, she was amazed to see that not one sugar cube was left in the silver bowl. They couldn't have used every one for sweetening tea.

She understood later when she was setting the table for dinner (not supper). The littles were down on all fours and in a huddle in the hall. A closer look showed that they were using a black ball-point to make spots on the hard white squares.

She said sternly, "I'm not buying lump sugar for you to make dice out of."

They looked up guiltily. "We won't use any more," they promised, and Brian added, "We can swap them for a lot of things."

Ah well, the littles were bound to be a cross.

She was proud of her tea, and she was proud of the dinner she served on the dining table by candlelight. She had made the entree she had thought so delicious and unusual in the McHarg home—Asparagus Metropolitan. "It's a meal in one," Mrs. McHarg said, "all you need with it is salad and dessert."

To make it Katie Rose had again toasted those beautifully white and symmetrical slices of baker's bread. She fitted a slice of ham over each, and over the ham laid the soft green logs of cooked frozen asparagus. She made a cheese sauce and poured over the individual servings on the plates. A green salad accompanied it, and for dessert she had only to thaw out two lemon pies from the dairy counter at Maplewood Mart.

The littles looked down at their plates, looked around the table bare of food, and Matt said, "But gee, Katie Rose, what've we got for waddin'?"

Ben nudged him to silence.

Stacy asked almost meekly when the meal was finished, "Would it be all right if I made some more toast, Katie Rose?"

She brought in butter and blackberry jam with it.

Liz said, "Ah, it's nice to have candles and flowers on the table."

"Seems funny to light candles when it isn't dark yet," Jill commented.

Ben quieted her too. "No remarks out of you, missy. Katie Rose is doing things the way she wants them."

The day was one of triumph for Katie Rose. Her only jolt came when she went to fix Ben's lunch for the next day. There was no bread. Good heavens, she had thought those six loaves would carry them well into the week. She threw on a sweater, and went hurrying to Wetzel's store for more.

The front door was already locked, but Papa Wetzel left his meat block to limp to it and open it for her. Mamma Wetzel said, "So you're buying bread, Katie Rose. You could hold a loaf of this baker's bread in one hand, and a slice of your mother's in the other, and I'll bet they'd weigh the same."

Mr. Wetzel was cutting meat off bones for grinding in the morning. He was very proud of his ground beef, and didn't like customers to ask for "hamburger." He turned to beam at Katie Rose. "You wait just a minute, and I'll give you some of these good bones to make a pot of soup like your mother does. The French teacher at the college is always after us for them. He knows that nothing makes as rich a stock as backbones."

Mother always said that too. "They flavor and body up a soup." But Katie Rose winced every time the Wetzels handed her a knobby package of them.

She drew a long breath. Now was the time for her to take her stand. "I won't be cooking up soup the way Mother does. I can buy soup mixes at the supermarket and make it in ten minutes."

They looked at her as though she had uttered a

sacrilege. She was conscious of the chill in the atmosphere as she paid for the bread and went out.

Ben came into the kitchen when she was fixing his lunch. "Katie Rose, would you mind putting in *three* sandwiches instead of two? I was hollow as a gourd by ten o'clock this morning and I had to eat one."

EIGHT

The Belford littles had a deep grievance against life. It was because they no longer had the run of the city dump.

Until the first of June, it had been open to any citizen, young or old, who cared to prowl among the discards and pick up whatever he or she desired. It was within bicycling distance of Hubbell Street, and had been a gold mine for the littles. Not only had they brought home the broken purple necklace Katie Rose had worn in the fashion show, and a cracked saucer they fed their white mice from, but also broken cigarette lighters, hub caps, bicycle parts—all treasure which they used for swapping among the young contingent.

Brian's prize possession was a broken-bladed sword on which he spent long hours with a whetstone, hoping to put a point back on it. Jill's prize was some bound-together leather squares, evidently a salesman's samples. These had high swapping value for fashioning into slingshots.

But Matt's find made him the most envied boy in all South Denver. He told the story over and over again. How he had been walking through the dump, and stooped to pick up what he thought was a marble. Instead it was a very realistic, oval-shaped glass eye.

"My soul and body!" Mother shuddered. "It gives me the creeps to think of you carrying around the glass eye of some dead man."

"He doesn't have to be dead," Ben said. "Somebody probably discarded that old-fashioned glass eye years ago and got one of the kind they use now. Now they're just thin little discs."

Matt's "Old Glassy," as he fondly called it, was so dear to him that he refused magnificent offers for trading.

But the first of June the city turned its ownership of the dumps over to individuals who could dispose of all the hapless discards as they saw fit. That was the end of the happy marauding. And life lost a certain excitement and charm for the littles.

They sat at the dinette table on Tuesday morning brooding over life's injustice while Katie Rose and Liz cleared away the breakfast dishes.

They were still there when Uncle Tim arrived from Bannon, and came swaggering into the kitchen. He was the husband of Mother's sister, Aunt Kitty, and the one who had to have his hot, homecooked meal at noon. He worked with Grandda on building contracts.

Uncle Tim's first greeting was for the disconsolate three. "How'd you like to bundle up a few duds and come out to Bannon with me? Kitty and I were talking about it. You can have yourselves a time with our boy. There're baseball games on every corner, and Bannon's got a new swimming pool. You can fish in the reservoir. How about it?"

The littles listened with bright, considering eyes, but didn't commit themselves.

Matt asked, "Can we take Cully with us and our—?"

"Not on your life. You know how your Aunt Kitty feels about four-legged critters."

The Belfords did know and often talked about it; how Aunt Kitty never allowed "her one," who was a little older than the twins, to own a dog or cat or even goldfish in a bowl.

Uncle Tim added, "But your gran's little Jersey had

a new calf a couple of nights ago. Your grandda said you could come over and help him milk, and feed the calf."

Katie Rose remembered that last Friday Grandda had mentioned that when Gran's cow came in fresh, he would have milk and cream pile up on him. She remembered with a pang that he had gone off without a "Bye, Bye, Blackbird" to her.

She poured Uncle Tim a cup of coffee. "You'll be glad to have these young hellions off your hands, won't you, Katie Rose? No reason why they can't spend the whole summer with us—or at least till your mother comes back. They'll be company for Grandda. They can spend the nights with him."

How many times had Katie Rose thought of those three as one of life's crosses? Yes, it would certainly simplify her nicer-living program, and yet—yet the house would be strangely lacking without them. She said, "It's up to them—whatever they want to do."

Jill asked, "Do they let anybody go to the junk yard in Bannon and help themselves?"

"Sure," boomed Uncle Tim. "Not only that, but your grandda and I have got our own junk yard with old lumber and broken-down equipment." He set down his coffee cup, moved to the door. "I have to pick up some hardware. You throw together some clothes and I'll swing by and pick you up."

The mention of the junk yards had evidently tipped the scales. The littles went scurrying up the stairs to pack.

Liz confided to Katie Rose, "I think Tim and Kitty are trying to make up for being so selfish. Him, and his hot meal at noon! Her, and her *one!* Kitty could have gone with Gran a lot easier than your mother with her job, and a big houseful. Dear Goodness, now I must be leaving for the dentist."

No one ever knew what went on in the heads of the littles. When Uncle Tim arrived for them, it developed that only two of the three were going. Spokesman Jill announced to Katie Rose and Uncle Tim, "One of us has to stay home because there's lots of things to see to."

The one to stay was the youngest, Brian. In all their eleven and a half years, the twins had never been separated.

The three were very vague when Katie Rose wanted to know what important matters had to be seen to. They mentioned the *Call* subscribers who still owed them for their papers—

"Just leave me the slips, and either Stacy or I will collect from them," Katie Rose said.

They muttered evasively about a boy named Louie who had a bicycle headlight he was going to swap. And there was some whispered injunction to Brian about going to a pet shop on the Boulevard.

But when the pickup drove off, Brian looked so small and unattached, and somehow forlorn, standing there with Cully—also looking unattached and forlorn—that Katie Rose said, "Ah, honey, you should have gone too."

He said stanchly, "Somebody has to stay home and take care of—just lots of things."

He mounted his bicycle and, with Cully following, was off.

The phone was ringing when Katie Rose went into the empty house. She raced to it and picked up the receiver.

"Katie Rose? This is Perry McHarg—do you remember me?"

As though she could forget that unfathomable, blunt-spoken Perry who would no doubt make his way in the hotel and restaurant management world. As though she had forgotten his invitation to lunch with him at the Golden Slipper. Her mind went racing ahead — Should she wear her fashion-show dress which he had already seen, or the coral-colored one he hadn't?

"Oh yes, Perry. How are you?"

He wasted no time on the amenities, but came right to the point—and it was not setting a date for the luncheon. "Do you have an extra room at your house? Carol's—Mrs. McHarg's—sister and her husband are arriving today from Nebraska. And she has to give them my room. It's too late for me to get into the men's dorm here on campus because it's filled now. The McHargs suggested my calling you. We thought, maybe with your mother gone, you might let me take her room."

Katie Rose started to say, "But Liz is in the alcove off her room, and Stacy has Mom's bed," when she thought of the littles' room. Only Brian was left, and he could sleep on the extra cot in Ben's room.

She said hesitantly, "Yes, we've got an extra room. The twins went to Bannon this morning."

The minute she said it she was overcome with near panic. Perry McHarg *here?* Oh no. She'd better backtrack—and fast.

But his businesslike voice was saying, "That's fine. I'll never be there for lunch. I like to go to different restaurants—and don't forget I want to take you, too. The fellows who board at the dorm, and just take breakfast and dinner, pay eighteen a week. Is that all right with you?"

"Well, yes—yes, that'll be all right."

"Would it be too soon for me to have dinner there this evening, and for you to have the room ready for tonight? Because Carol's folks are due sometime today."

"Yes—I mean no, it won't be too soon."

"Good, Katie Rose. I appreciate it. I'll come after Marketing class. It's out at five, but we usually have coffee and a jam session afterwards." The phone clicked at his end.

For a moment or two she leaned weakly against the wall. Perry McHarg *here?* It was frightening, but it was challenging too. She'd show him that the Belford menage was no step down from the McHargs'.

And then she was lifted by a wave of exultation. He had noticed her. He had remembered her. He could have picked up the morning paper and found a list of boarding houses—but he had *wanted* to come here. He had wanted to see more of her.

Eighteen dollars a week. Why, that plus Ben's ten and Liz's ten, plus the backlog Mother had left— She would be rolling in money. And six was the perfect number to cook for, and set a table for.

She was galvanized into action. She took three Cornish hens out of the freezer compartment in the refrigerator to thaw. She raced up the stairs to the littles' room.

One look at it and her heart dropped to her flapping sandals. She was seeing it not through her eyes, but through those opaque and critical eyes of her boarder-to-be. She was comparing it to the McHarg guest room with its rust-colored carpeting, built-in desk, closet with sliding doors, bed light and desk lamp.

Like the other upstairs rooms, the littles' was a corner one with a window on each outer wall. It held a double bunk bed for Matt and Brian, and a single bed for Jill.

Last winter Mother had decided that Jill should no longer share a room with her brothers, and had moved her into the alcove off her room. The plan hadn't worked. Mother got home from Guido's Gay Nineties any time between midnight and two. Jill had to scramble out at five to carry on her paper route with the boys. She was supposed to get up quietly and slip out without waking Mother, but Jill was not the quiet type. So she had gone back to her happy habitat, and Ben had compromised by flanking her bed with a high chest of drawers.

Mother had once, in one of her inspired flurries, decided to do over their room. With a Mexican decor in mind, she painted the walls pale blue. There were many imperfections in the plaster from the dart games and bows and arrows the littles received at Christmases, and over the worst of them Mother had tacked splashy Mexican posters of bullfights. She had bought white curtains at a rummage sale, and stitched ruffles of red calico on them. She had meant to dot the floor with red shag rugs, but money—or rather the lack of it— had stopped her.

All this Katie Rose's eyes took in, and then came

back to rest on the sourest note in the room. Not the bowl piled with flat rocks under which a turtle, no bigger than a half-dollar, crouched. It was the white mice in their homemade edifice which resembled a misshapen Quonset hut.

The littles had filled a discarded cupboard drawer with dirt, and had built up a rounded screen for the top. They had labored to cut a door in the screen which fastened by means of a fence staple and safety pin, and through which they reached food and water to the inmates.

The mice themselves, named Gertie and George, were not in sight. When Katie Rose, the intruder, had walked into the room they had hurriedly flicked themselves into a burrow in the dirt. The littles could bring them out by low chirping sounds and fond murmurs of, "Come out, George—don't be afraid, Gertie."

Katie Rose's baleful eyes took in the wilted cabbage and celery leaves and shriveled bits of carrots. A Mason jar top held murky water, and the cracked saucer from the dump held cornflakes. The whole family, and especially Katie Rose, forever scolded the littles about this odorous addition to their room.

She glanced into Ben's room. It was the smallest of all the four bedrooms and, while there was room for Brian on the extra cot—and even for the bowl with turtle—there was no room for a mice Quonset.

With Perry McHarg moving in, the white mice had to go.

She tugged at the unwieldy cage to lift it off what could serve the new boarder as a desk. The drawer with its half-foot of dirt seemed to weigh a ton, and the built-up screen top made it awkward to get a grip on. It tilted in her arms, spilling dirt into her sandals. One white mouse darted out of its hole. The other showed only its whiskers and pink beady eyes—and then both disappeared.

She struggled down the stairs with the box. It was all she could do to get herself and her armsful through the back door. She set it on the ground and straightened up. Whew!—it was a messy, smelly contraption.

She was shaking dirt out of her sandals when she saw two little boys passing the Belford side gate. They were pulling a wagon with a few papers in it, and one of them called to her, "Have you got any newspapers to give us for our paper drive?"

She shook her head. And then on a sudden inspiration, she called back, "Hey, would either of you like this cage with two white mice in it? I'll give them to you." She was telling herself: The twins at Bannon will be so busy swimming and fishing and going through the junk yard, they'll never give them a thought. In case they raised a ruckus when they came back, she'd buy them another pair.

The little boys stopped. One said in amazement, "You mean you'll *give* them to us? They cost a quarter apiece at the Pet Shop."

"Yes, you can have them. Just take them with you," she said hurriedly.

She even helped them load the Quonset onto the small wagon. They started off with much arguing as to which one should pull the wagon, which one steady the load, and which one should take the mice home with him.

Katie Rose didn't tarry. She had too much to do.

Armed with broom and mop, she went back up the stairs. Jill's bed could be removed. She took it apart herself. When Stacy returned from school, the two of them could carry the dismembered parts up in the attic. And when Ben got home from work, she'd have him help her take off the top bed on the double bunk, which would leave only a three-quarter one for Perry McHarg.

She didn't hear Stacy come in, but the unmistakable smell of nail polish came sifting up the stairs. Looking down, she saw Stacy on the bottom step applying polish to her toenails.

"Stacy, I need you to help me."

"Just a sec. Yesterday when I was out at Coral Sands *every* girl there had her toenails painted. I just scringed because mine were bare—"

"*Cringed*," Katie Rose corrected.

"This is Jungle Rose. Come on down and I'll do yours."

"I'm too busy. The twins went to Bannon with Uncle Tim—maybe for the whole summer. I'm moving Brian into Ben's room, and cleaning out the littles'. We're going to have a boarder. And guess who? Mr. McHarg's cousin—Perry McHarg."

"How old is he? I mean is he too old to fall for my fatal charm? Or have you staked a claim on him?"

"He's going on twenty, and he's had two years of college—"

"Going on twenty! Practically doddering. You can have him."

"Come on, Stacy, and help me carry the bed parts up to the attic."

Together they bumped headboards and footboards up the narrow stairs. The mattress was the hardest to manage. Stacy said, "Is this McHarg a G.I.P. or something we have to knock ourselves out for?"

Leave it to Stacy to mix V.I.P. for Very Important Person with the G.O.P. of the Republican party. But Katie Rose at that moment was too short of breath to correct her.

They came down the attic stairs, and Katie Rose halted in the bathroom door and panted out, "I'm going to get towel sets in different colors so each one

will have his own—his means *her* too. I thought of
brown for Ben, and green for you. And what color do
you think would be nice for the littles?"

"Red," Stacy said promptly, "so all their bloody
battles won't show on the towel. My bloomin' eye,
separate towels for each and every." And she sang out,

> *We must put on the dog*
> *For this Perry McHogg.*

"Don't you dare call him McHogg. But just look
at this dreary mess. The McHarg bathroom is like a
rainbow."

"You wouldn't be having a rainbow round your
shoulder, and your head is in the clouds for him,
would you, Katie Rose?"

She mustn't let Stacy guess that her head was
slightly in the clouds because he had remembered her.
She said on a shrug, "He's the rooted-to-the-ground
type. All he can think about is price tags and hotel
equipment. But I don't want him thinking we're poor
white trash."

"How long's he going to board here?"

"I didn't ask him. I think this Hotel and Restaurant
Management school is for seven or eight weeks. I'm
not sure when it started."

The doorknocker sounded, which meant that Bruce
Seerie was calling for Stacy. She started down the

stairs, but stopped halfway, and turned an anxious face upward. "Look, Sis, if Ben gets home before I do, and if he says anything about my going swimming with Bruce, you tell him that tomorrow afternoon I'm going to the library and read, read, read for my make-up lit."

"You tell him yourself."

Katie Rose was a little worried herself about Ben, the watchdog of the family. Maybe she should have told Perry McHarg she would have to talk to Ben first. But no, Mother had left the running of the house to her. And if she wanted to take on all the extra work of a boarder in order to make money so they could all live better—well, that was her own house-running business.

NINE

Katie Rose, in a flurry of excitement, tucked her mother's twenty-dollar bills in her billfold, tucked herself into Miguel's Triumph, and set out for the May Company in the University Hills shopping center. Once there, she made straight for the linen department.

And in the linen department, she told the first saleslady who came forward she was interested in bath sets. The affable clerk assured her that now, with their summer white sale in progress, was the right time to stock up. Here was a wonderful buy—their regular five-dollar bath towel in Empire Brocade, reduced to only three ninety-nine.

Katie Rose did mental arithmetic. The bath and hand towel with matching wash cloth would come to about seven dollars. No, not the Empire Brocade when she had so many sets to buy.

But bath sets in Royal Symphony added up to a mere five forty-seven. She chose Stacy's in Dynasty Green. Castilian Red for the littles, and Mocha for Ben. She hesitated between Antique Gold and Lemon Yellow for their boarder, but decided on yellow as more of a rainbow shade. For herself, she took a luscious lavender called Persian Lilac. What shade for Liz? She thought of her rosy cheeks, and added three matched pieces of Siamese Pink.

Oh, and Mother! It would never do for her to come home and not be represented in the rainbow bath. This Ming Turquoise would be so right for someone with sparkly blue-green eyes.

"Anything in bath mats?" the clerk queried.

Katie Rose had only to finger the velvety pile of the bath mats and compare them to the washed-out, bedraggled one beside their bathtub at home to say yes. And because she was still thinking of blue-green eyes, she chose one in turquoise (three ninety-nine).

Rainbows came high. Forty-three dollars and thirteen cents, including tax.

She was walking out of the department with her

huge bundle when she saw a clerk displaying a bright red shag rug for another customer. Katie Rose stopped. This rug was larger than the one small and wrinkled one in their guest room. And it was a perfect match for the red calico trim on the curtains and the bullfighter's cape in the posters on the wall. It was also non-skid. After all, a paying boarder deserved a rug underfoot. No, *rugs,* because if one cost seven ninety-five, you were saving money to buy two for fifteen dollars. She bought two.

Heavily burdened as she was, there was still another *must.* These were iced-tea days, and the Belford cupboard contained only a few odds and ends of unmatched chipped glasses.

Talk about luck! She ran into a sale in the china and glassware department too. Mexican blue or amber glasses and matching plates, hexagonal in shape, for only eighty-eight cents each. Remembering the blue glassware on the McHarg table, she chose amber so that Perry McHarg wouldn't think her a copycat.

Even though there would be only six at the table, she again thought of her mother's return. And standing there with one of the plates in her hand, her fondest and loveliest dream took over. Mother and Gran returning from Ireland, weary and homesick. And Mother sitting at the table, so beautifully set and with a delicious, different, eye-catching menu set before her. Mother would look at her and breathe in heartfelt awe, "Katie Rose, you're a miracle worker, no less."

There would be no more chuckles about her thinking she could run a house better than her mother.

Katie Rose bought eight glasses, and the matching pitcher which was two forty-nine. And eight plates. She stood then, admiring the table that had been set to display the amber glassware. The clerk said, "You see how the green place mats bring out the amber. They tend to be dull without a bright color with them."

She bought eight lacy woven place mats, also Mexican, and in a flower design.

A boy from the stock room had to help carry out all her purchases and load them into the Triumph. She could barely see over them as she drove out of the parking lot.

At home, she took the price tags off the towels for arranging on the racks. Their two racks couldn't begin to accommodate them. Towel racks she could get at the dime store on the Boulevard.

But first, because the towels looked so new and store-creased, and because she didn't want Perry McHarg to know she had gone rushing out to buy them, she took the whole batch down to the wringer-type machine in the basement. She gave them a quick sudsing, rinsing, and hung them out on the line. Thank heaven, for the bright sun and whipping breeze.

Again she got in the Triumph and, this time, turned it toward the Boulevard.

Why was a store called the Five and Dime when you couldn't buy a blessed thing there for a nickel or a dime? A towel rack with a glass rod was a dollar thirty-nine. She needed three. Yes, and more toothbrush holders. Only one hung in the Belford bath with space for five dangling brushes, which meant that there were always extra brushes lining the washbowl or dropping onto the floor. But these holders that held two brushes, and had a shelf for toothpaste, would be perfect to fasten over the towel racks.

She bought three of those too.

She was waiting for her change when her name was called loudly through the store. It was Rita Flood at Cosmetics, two counters over. "Did you find the pattern?" she was shouting.

Katie Rose, her mind on many things, could only stare at her blankly. Rita refreshed her memory, "For that dress you made in sewing that I'm going to make one just like."

Katie Rose shook her head absently. Rita was informing her and everyone else in the store, "I've got a swell job. I'm working three nights a week at the

Pant—and I'm going to work now." She called back from the door as she left, "If I can't get the stuff to make it this payday, I will the next."

So Rita had the job at the Pant that Dr. Kincaid wouldn't let Jeanie accept. Rita's folks would waste no time worrying about her getting home at midnight.

All thoughts of Rita faded from Katie Rose's mind when the clerk gave her her change and she put it in her billfold. She looked closer at its contents in jolted disbelief. Why no, that couldn't be right. She couldn't have only *one* twenty-dollar bill left, plus some silver. She must have lost some.

Mother had left her seven twenties and a ten. Her mind backtracked. Two of the twenties had gone to the cashier at Maplewood Mart. Two *and* a five for the towels and bath mat. Then she had seen the red shag rug— And then she had gone to chinaware—

No, she hadn't *lost* any.

But there was no reason to panic. She would have board money coming in every week. Thirty-eight dollars would serve beautifully for a family of six. She breathed easier.

She didn't dare wait for Ben's installing the towel racks and toothbrush holders. She wrestled with screw driver and screws herself, and ended up with two towel racks that didn't fit tight to the wall, and a gouged thumb. She was feeling pushed and harried, when

Brian came up the stairs with Cully at his heels.

But again his very aloneness tugged at her heart. She took her maimed thumb out of her mouth, and called to him, "Brian, honey, you won't mind sleeping in Ben's room, will you? I had a chance to take a boarder—just think, he'll pay eighteen a week—and so I cleaned up your room for him."

"Oh, that's all right." He glanced in his old room, and then went to Ben's. He came hurrying to the bathroom door to ask, "What'd you do with George and Gertie?"

"Brian, that box was the smelliest old thing, and the dirt always running out of it—and it was so big there wasn't room—"

"Where are they?"

"I gave them to a little boy that'll give them a good home."

He stared at her out of stricken, unbelieving eyes. "You gave away our mice," he breathed. "But I promised Matt I'd look after them. That's why I didn't go to Bannon. Because somebody had to stay home—because Aunt Kitty would never let us take them out there."

"Oh now, Brian! Matt and Jill will never give a thought to those mice. And it'd be different if I actually got rid of them. But this little boy was so tickled to get them—you could tell he'd be good to them."

"Who was he?"

"I don't know. There were two of them—and they were collecting papers."

He stood there, crushed and wordless. Matt and Jill, she realized, would have found words—and plenty of them—to reproach her. She defended herself, "How did I know those white mice were so precious? You never said a word about your staying home to nurse them along."

"Nobody else liked the mice but us," he said in a small voice. "That's why none of us didn't say nothing about them."

She left him there while she hurried down to get the towels off the line. She was sorry he was grieved about the mice. But then children soon forget, she told herself.

Ben was late coming home from work. The new boarder, with his typewriter, suitcase, briefcase, and an armful of books, arrived first. Katie Rose escorted him up the stairs and to his room. She explained that Ben would remove the top half of the bunk—

"No, don't bother," Perry McHarg said. "I'm used to sleeping in a double bunk at home."

He was taller than she remembered. Perhaps it was the square set to his shoulders and jaw that made him seem short, compared to the stripling upshooting of both Ben and Miguel.

"I hope you like the room," she ventured.

"I like it fine." His smile was even more warm and folksy than she remembered. But oh, those all-encompassing eyes of his behind the glasses. She had a feeling that he knew every plaster hole under the bullfighters, and even that she had spent money she shouldn't have for new rugs to give the room a lift. He wanted to hurry back to the university and join in the marketing discussion, he told her. He asked her what time dinner was served, and was off again in his station wagon.

Such a businesslike young man!

Ben returned, his face an even deeper scarlet, his work boots so encrusted with cement he left them at the back door. But he was happy because he had worked an extra hour at time and a half.

Tea this day was not a Belford mansion one but a hasty and sketchy affair with Liz helping. Ben had to hear all about the twins going off with Uncle Tim, and the shift in sleeping arrangements because of the boarder. Katie Rose emphasized the munificent board money she would receive.

Liz said, "Ah, it'll be nice to have him. I was afraid the table would seem lacking with the twins gone."

Katie Rose briefed Liz, Ben, and a very quiet Brian on the color of their towels in the rainbow bath. She didn't want any loud exclamations of, "For goshsakes, what are all the towels for?" in Perry McHarg's hearing.

Ben's sunburned forehead puckered. "You didn't spend that backlog Mom left for all this fancy stuff, did you?"

"Just part of it." Thank heaven, he couldn't see that lone twenty left in her billfold. "But you don't need to worry, Ben. I'll get along just fine."

She got off with his tired, perhaps skeptical, shrug. "I promised Mom I'd keep still as long as I got enough to eat. That reminds me; I guess you'd better put *four* sandwiches in my lunch. I feel pretty caved-in about three in the afternoon too."

Stacy did not get off so easily. He took one look at her wet hair when she came in, and said, "Is that your idea of making up your grades—getting a peeling sunburn out at Coral Sands?"

"Tomorrow, I'm going down to the library and get *A Doll's House* and read it. Golly, you'd wonder about anyone writing a big long play about a doll's house. I've got the best stuff for sunburn, Ben—"

Ben was not to be deflected. "Either you tell your buddy, Bruce, or I'll tell him that three afternoons a week at Coral Sands is all your time allows. You're not going to summer school just because your hair is curly and your eyes are blue."

A chastened Stacy helped Katie Rose unpack the

amber glassware and set the table. But Stacy could
not stay chastened for long. "Just like downtown!"
she said ebulliently, as she arranged the lacy mats and
set on each a six-sided plate.

Again Katie Rose beamed with happy triumph
throughout that first dinner for her boarder. How
could he help but be impressed?

"Cornish hens," mused Liz. "Sure, I never heard of
them before. And rice for stuffing. I always used
bread."

The boarder interrupted his talk with Ben to ask,
"How much do you pay for a package of wild rice?"

"I didn't notice," she said loftily.

She had noticed one disappointing thing though. It
had said right on the frilly aluminum-foil pan containing frozen spinach soufflé, SERVES FOUR. Yet the two
she had heated in the oven barely served the six at the
table. Evidently the four it was supposed to serve
didn't have Belford appetites.

Two glorious weeks went by. Breakfasts with a
choice of dry breakfast food. Katie Rose didn't stick to
bacon and eggs. She treated her family and the hotel
and restaurant management student to chipped beef on
toast, or sausages wrapped in biscuits (canned).

A small vase filled with pansies sat on the table
every morning. Liz saw to that. The scattered pansies
she had fitted back into the broken box had thrived on

the sunny windowsill of the dinette. And each time Liz picked them, she murmured, "I'd just like to know why that vixen threw a box of pansies that cost eighty-nine cents at Miguel's camera."

Yes, Katie Rose's breakfasts and dinners all but out-McHarged the McHargs'.

Perry took her to luncheon at the Golden Slipper. She wore her coral-colored linen cut on princess lines, with each gore touched off with tiny white ruffles. (Miguel always called it her petunia dress.) She borrowed her mother's pearls.

But her escort had eyes for everything in the dining room except his luncheon companion. His X-ray eyes studied the bill of fare.

"Do you like red snapper, Katie Rose?"

"I've never tasted it."

"How about trying it? I want to see how long it takes them to fill your order so I'll know whether it's frozen or fresh."

He ordered for himself the special luncheon which was meat loaf, garden vegetables, and apple pie.

He had X-ray taste buds as well. "Bread crumbs and eggs in the meat loaf, but good seasoning. Fresh asparagus. And the pie isn't canned apples—they're fresh green ones. I'll bet their buyer is at the market at dawn to get vegetables and fruits."

"Was my red snapper frozen?"

He nodded. "A fillet like that would broil in twelve or fifteen minutes if it were fresh. It was thirty-five minutes getting here."

"Why don't you go out and talk to the cook?" she asked sarcastically. He certainly hadn't carried on any conversation with her.

"Chef," he corrected. "I'll do that another time. This time, I wanted to get customer reaction."

Another noontime he took her to the Red Ox, which specialized in beef and whose air was heavy with the smoky haze of steaks broiled over charcoal. This time she wore her fashion-show dress with purple accessories. He didn't notice whether the beads did anything for her eyes or not.

But he noticed the size and thickness of the steaks piled beside the open broiler; he felt the texture of the red-checked luncheon cloth. He commented as he ate his steak, "It's not Grade A, but they know how to age it and cook it."

He still puzzled Katie Rose. He could flash her his wonderful warming smile that made her feel he saw *her* and liked what he saw. And the next minute he'd ask her what make pressure cooker they had.

"I don't know. Mom has an old one she used for beans and stews. I haven't used it since she left."

The family liked him. Liz made a fuss over him. Stacy called him Eff Ex, short for Efficiency Expert.

Ben and he talked about college courses. Little Brian showed him the foreshortened sword he'd found in the city dump, and Perry McHarg smuggled out of the school's kitchen a huge rough-edged steel for putting a better point on it.

Two postcards had come from Ireland. On the one showing Blarney Castle, Mother wrote, "Aunt Nellie rallied when we came. She doesn't mind my smoking. Rain every day. I miss you all." On the next card, picturing a jaunting car in Killarney, she wrote, "Aunt Nellie won't hear of going to the hospital or leaving her own home. We're trying to get one of the Callanan connections to come and look after her. Ask Pearl what color sweater she'd like."

Pearl was one of Mother's "give a little, take a little" circle of friends. Once when Pearl moved into a drab apartment, Mother found time to paint the walls for her. The littles ran her errands. Pearl reciprocated by giving the Belfords the bakery imperfects—a pie, slightly runny, or cup cakes that baked lopsided. This was another thing that tried Katie Rose's soul.

Miguel wrote from Washington on his father's typewriter. They were both putting in long hours on the book manuscript. He added, "I've decided not to be a writer. There should be easier ways of making a living. Write to me, Petunia."

From Bannon came a grimy postcard to Brian from

Jill, whose spelling was on a par with Stacy's pronunciation:

> *We cach fish in the reservore onley most*
> *of them are succers. send us oure share of*
> *the monny you colecked becaus Matt has*
> *got a traide hes workin on.*

As yet Brian had been unable to collect from the will-of-the-wisp woman who still owed for two months' subscription to the *Call*. He would have sent the twins all of the dollar seventy-five he had collected from another customer, but Katie Rose insisted that he keep his third of it. A dollar seventeen went to the two in Bannon.

Life would have been flawless for Katie Rose but for two things—or rather, two people dear to her heart. Brian. He hadn't mentioned the absent mice since that fateful day. She told herself that he wandered about like a lost soul because the twins were gone.

"Look, honey, why don't you go out to Bannon on the bus?" she urged. "I'll pay your fare. You'd have fun."

Was that a glimmer of pain in his eyes? "I don't want to go to Bannon," he said.

Every morning he set forth on his bicycle with Cully following.

The other flaw was Jeanie Kincaid. She was touchy and unpredictable these days. On Monday, Tuesday, and Friday she worked at the clinic where Scott Kincaid, M.D. was listed among the doctors. Sometimes she was the old Jeanie, complete as to twinkle, swift giggle, and the wisdom that had helped Katie Rose over many a rough spot. She would stop off at the Belfords' on her way home from work, and drink iced tea out of the amber glasses.

But she was still resentful of her father's tight rein. Once when Ben was cross-examining Stacy as to whether she had read *A Doll's House,* Jeanie flung out, "Oh, don't be so bossy, Ben. You sound just like Dad."

Another time she muttered with pent-up vehemence, "Katie Rose, I just wish I knew *why* that washed-out blond bolted for cover each time she saw me."

"It's because she owes your—"

"No. I went all over the file of Dad's uncollectable accounts. The cards list their age and occupation. Not one of them fits her."

Again Katie Rose was at an uneasy loss for words.

TEN

Two beautiful weeks and two days passed, and then on
a Wednesday evening, just when June had another
day to go, the telephone rang. Katie Rose answered.
The call was from Bannon.

Grandda O'Byrne's voice said, "This you, Katie
Rose?"

"And me, Stacy. I'm on the upstairs extension.
How are you getting along with our scalawags?"

Grandda paused briefly before he said, "That's just
what I'm calling about. I'll be bringing them home
tomorrow. I thought it'd be better after all that's
happened."

"After all that's— Why, what happened?" Katie Rose gasped.

Stacy cut in, "I'll bet I can guess. A big free-for-all." And Ben, who had come into the hall and was standing close enough to hear, muttered, "I was afraid they wouldn't hit it off with Kitty's one."

Grandda chuckled ruefully. "You're right, it was a big free-for-all. It got going when they were fishing today. And don't be asking me who hit who first. The story the twins tell doesn't jibe at all with the way Kitty's one puts it."

"Did anybody get hurt?"

"They all got bunged up while fists and fishing poles were swinging. And in the fracas, Matt got a fishhook stuck in him—"

"Oh good heavens! Where?"

"On his cheek, close to his eye. But he's all right. I took him to the doctor right away, and he gave him a tetanus shot. He wants to look at it again tomorrow. So I've got the two of them here with me. Soon as I'm through work tomorrow, I'll bring them in. Kitty's pretty hot under the collar. You know how she is about her one. Wait a minute, Matt wants to talk to Brian."

Brian listened to quite an outpouring from his wounded brother in Bannon. He said only, "You did?" and that was all. He replaced the phone, looking pale and shaken.

Katie Rose said, "I guess you're glad they're coming back."

"No. No, I don't want to see them."

"You don't! Why? What did Matt say?"

Brian wet dry lips, swallowed. "He's got—he traded for—for a real swell cage for Gertie and George. He says it'll hang up on the wall, and it's made out of copper wire—something like a bird cage. He said it was made for a hamster, and it's got a runway and a little house in it—and all sorts of things."

Katie Rose said over her wave of guilt, "Brian, I'll take you to that pet shop the very first thing in the morning. And we'll get two more white mice."

Brian shook his head numbly. "It's Gertie and George, Matt got it for. Matt and Jill would know the minute they looked at any new mice they weren't Gertie and George. Because George has a kinkly tail— he's the only white mouse that has—and Matt said he bet his tail got caught in a door or something. And Gertie has a kinda gray spot by her ear."

"Well, Brian, *you* don't have to feel bad. You tell Matt and Jill—no, I'll tell them—that I gave the mice away. Then they'll be mad at *me*."

"They left me to take care of them," he said wanly. "And now they're coming home—and Matt's got a bandage all over one side of his face. He can't hardly see out of one eye."

"What else did Matt say?" Stacy asked.

"He said this kid out at Bannon that had the copper cage wouldn't swap it for all of Jill's leather pieces and a power screw driver Grandda gave Matt because it kept slipping—or with even the money I sent. He wouldn't swap until Matt threw in Old Glassy—" his voice broke. "That's what made Kitty's one mad, Matt said—because he wanted Old Glassy hisself."

So even Matt's precious Old Glassy had been sacrificed for the copper cage to house the white mice. Katie Rose suggested hopefully, "Maybe if we bought hamsters, Brian—they're cute. I'll bet Matt would like hamsters."

He didn't deign to answer that. He started for the stairs, but turned back to utter his first reproach to Katie Rose, "You ought've asked that boy with the wagon what his name was."

"He takes things to heart so," Liz sighed.

Katie Rose said remorsefully, "I *should* have asked those kids who they were."

"I'm baby-sitting at the Novaks' this evening," Stacy said. "I'll ask those kids if they know *any* boy that was on a paper drive."

Perry McHarg came down the stairs. "Brian was telling me about the twins coming back. Matt can have his upper bunk, but will you have a bed for Jill?"

"We'll manage," Katie Rose said, close to tears.

He moved to her and took her arm. "Come on, Katie Rose, and go out with me. There's a motel at the edge of town with an outdoor cafe where they dance every evening."

"Yes, go on, childeen," urged Liz. "No use grieving over what can't be helped."

"It's all very informal," Perry said. "What you've got on will be all right."

What she had on was a pink eyelet which she and Stacy both wore. As though Perry McHarg would notice whether she wore gold lamé or gunnysacking. As though, right now, she gave a hoot. If it hadn't been for him, she would never have grabbed up that odorous mouse Quonset and shoved it off on the first small humans who came her way.

Stacy followed her upstairs. "Perry says to wear a wrap because the tables are close to the swimming pool and it'll be chilly." She reached in the closet and drew out a short blond and fuzzy jacket. "Why don't you live it up, and wear your Prom Night, Katie Rooo?" Stacy lifted the transparent covering of the wrap and snuggled her cheek against it, "Um-mm, it's so luscious, so seductious."

"*Seductive,*" Katie Rose corrected absently.

This satin-lined wrap that looked like fur had been a gift to Katie Rose from her wealthy Belford aunt. It was her most cherished possession. But it went with the heart-fluttery gaiety of going to a prom with heels and a corsage. "No, I'll just take a sweater," Katie Rose said this troubled evening.

In the garden of what was called Thc Coach and Four, Katie Rose sat at a small table across from Perry McHarg and drank Coke, and shivered now and then under her white sweater.

"You're worried about Matt, aren't you?"

"Not about him. He's always getting bunged up. It's Brian. I wish I hadn't given the mice away. I wish I could get them back."

They danced. Strange that tonight, when her mind was on other things, he should be more—well, attentive. "You're sweet, Katie Rose. You know something? It's always kind of worried me because I didn't feel as protective toward the female of the species as I thought I should. But toward you I do. I have a strong desire to keep you from getting hurt."

She didn't answer. The dance was almost ended when she exclaimed suddenly, "Duffy! I remember now. I mean, when those two kids were starting off, the one that was holding the mouse box on said, 'D'you think your dad will let you keep them, Duffy?' "

"Good, Katie Rose, good. You tell Brian and he ought to be able to run down a kid named Duffy. And you tell Matt that he can hang his copper mansion in our room. I wouldn't mind a couple of mice around."

"Thanks, Perry," she said gratefully.

The house was dark and quiet when they returned and tiptoed up the stairs. She thought of waking Brian and telling him what her memory had dredged up. But that would mean waking Ben in the nearby bed, and Ben needed his sleep. She would wait until morning.

Before dawn, Katie Rose wakened from a heavy, troubled sleep. Something was wrong. She looked at the clock on the vanity. It was only five. What had wakened her? Why, it was Cully, whining and yelping, and now and then letting out a moan of distress. She realized that she had been hearing it through her sleep for hours.

She got up and looked out the window. In the faint light she could see that the dog was tied to the clothes post. Who in the world could have tied him there? And why? Good heavens, the fool dog could easily choke himself the way he kept circling the pole and shortening the rope.

She pulled on a robe, and raced down the steps in her bare feet, and out the back door. The dog was so helplessly enmeshed in the rope, and so excited at sight of her, that there was no untying him. She had to run back to the kitchen for a knife to cut him loose.

The frayed rope dangling from his collar, Cully ran

to the side gate whimpering in distress. She called to him sternly, and he came back to her. But he only stood, quivering and beseeching, and then headed for the gate again.

He wanted to follow someone. A dark thought kept tugging at Katie Rose's sleepy mind. Oh no—no, it couldn't be— But she bundled her robe close about her, raced inside the house and up the stairs and made for Ben's room where Brian slept on the small cot.

By the gray light of dawn she could see that it was empty. She even felt it to make sure. She leaned over Ben, and shook him, "Ben, where's Brian? Look, he isn't in his bed."

Ben jerked up, all touseled hair and heavy eyes, blinking as he looked toward the bed. "Turn on the light," he said, his voice thick with sleep.

He reached for his T-shirt on a chair by the bed and thrust his long arms into it. He sat up staring at the empty cot. "I went to bed early—and slept like a log. He hadn't come to bed yet. Ask Stacy or Liz—maybe they know something about the kid."

Liz was already awake. She seemed to have a sensitive antenna that told her when something was wrong. She said as Katie Rose came in, "Is it the little boy-een?"

Katie Rose nodded. "He's gone."

They wakened Stacy, and talked in alarmed whispers because of the sleeping boarder. Stacy shook her head. She had come home from the Novaks' at eleven, and Cully wasn't tied up then—

Ben joined them. Stacy was bending over to reach for a tennis shoe when she straightened and said, "Sarge Quinleaven, I bet."

She hurried on, "You all remember Sarge that sat next to Brian at school? And remember how the Quinleavens go every summer to their farm—or a sort of foothill ranch—near Winthrop? And remember how Sarge wanted Brian to come with them? And how they talked about a creek where they could pan gold—?"

"Good lord, Stacy," Ben interruped, "Winthrop is thirty—maybe thirty-two miles east of here. What makes you think he'd head for there? Did he say anything?"

"No. But before I left for the Novaks', he was hunting for that old gold pan. I don't think he found it though."

"Did he say anything to you, Liz?"

"Winthrop!" Liz ran a hand over her sleep-flushed face. "No, he never said a word to me. He poked around like a sad little wraith all evening. But when I was emptying the garbage, I heard him asking the old gentleman next door how you'd get onto the Winthrop road. I didn't think a thing about it at the time."

"You take Colfax Avenue out of town," Ben said, "and then branch off toward the south—"

"Oh, God have mercy! The poor unhappy boyeen."

It was the first clue of any kind they could fasten to, and Katie Rose seized it eagerly. "I'll go after him. He mustn't have left till after eleven-thirty, because when Perry and I came home Cully was in the hall." She said it from the doorway of her room as she slid her feet into sandals.

"I'll go with you," Ben said. "Maybe we can find him before it's time for me to go to work."

"No, Ben—no. I want to go—by myself. You know why he left. Because I gave the mice away, and he doesn't want to be here when the twins come home. I—well, I just want to find him, and then we'll work at tracking down the mice. I remembered last night that one of the little boys called the other one Duffy."

"The poor child takes things so to heart," Liz murmured again.

Mother had said the same thing the night before she left, "I don't feel right about leaving Brian. He's our baby. And he takes things so to heart—" And Katie Rose had said, "I'll take care of Brian, don't you worry."

In a matter of seconds, Katie Rose was dressed in a striped blouse and blue shorts. She wouldn't even wait for the coffee Liz was putting on.

They all followed her out to Miguel's Triumph at the curb. Ben gave her parting advice, "Don't bother looking for him as you go through town. He's well on the road by now. Check any trucks you pass. They're not supposed to pick up passengers, but some of them do. I hope it won't be a wild goose chase."

Katie Rose turned on the motor, calling to them, "Hold on to Cully. Be just like the crazy dog to follow me."

She lost no time in reaching Colfax Avenue, the main artery that ran east and west through Denver. She turned east on it. Nor had the sun lost any time in coming up. As she drove into it, she had to shield her eyes with her palm. Slowly, watchfully, she drove past the huge, sprawling, fenced-in Veterans' Hospital.

Beyond it was a filling station. A truck with a horse trailer was stopped there for gas, and for a minute hope lifted high under her ribs. She could see ahead that a boy—about Brian's size—was reaching through the trailer slats to feed or pet the horse inside it. She slowed to almost a stop. It wasn't a boy at all, but a girl of about ten in Levi's and visored cap, who was evidently accompanying her father to some horse show.

A few miles farther on she saw the sign WIN-THROP with an arrow pointing to the road that angled off south and east.

It was a relief not to be driving directly into the sun's glare. She drove slowly on this less-traveled road, her eyes searching not only the ochre ribbon ahead but on both sides of it. An up-and-down hilly, treeless country. All the while she drove, she was trying hard to concentrate on any remarks those two little boys with the wagon had exchanged.

How could a small boy with one pair of legs have come so many miles since around midnight last night? Of course he could have caught a late bus to Colfax, and then connected with another which took him beyond the Veterans' Hospital. He might have flagged a ride. She wished now that Ben had come with her. What would she do if she reached Winthrop without finding Brian? How would she locate the ranch where Sarge Quinleaven's folks lived?

Prairie land lay on each side of the raised road, with barbed wire fences running parallel to it.

She was staring ahead to the unbroken rows of fence posts when her senses suddenly quickened. It was the sight of what looked from this distance to be a post casting a shadow *toward* the road, and not away from it as the others did. Her eyes riveted to that one post as she drew nearer—

Yes, it had to be a human being, because a post didn't cast a shadow with a blob of green that could be a little boy's shirt. A post didn't cast a shadow with

something that the sun caught on and glistened and
which could be that broken sword Brian spent so many
hours on to shape into a point.

There he was! He was sitting, his back against the
post and his feet stretched out in front of him. His
tawny blond head was low on his chest, and he slept
wearily in the bright sun. He looked so small, so lost,
so *defenseless*, in spite of the sword across his knees,
that a sob caught in Katie Rose's throat.

He didn't even hear her stop the car. She went
stumbling down the embankment and through the
weed-grown ditch in such haste that she fell and, without intending to, let out a cry as her bare knees grazed
the hard soil. Her cry wakened him.

She dropped down beside him and sobbed out,
"Brian, my dearest own—I was so worried—"

He held himself stiff in her arms. He didn't look
at her, but kept his eyes on the road ahead. "I'm not
going back with you. I was just resting for a little
while. It's not very much farther to Sarge's."

"Look, honey, I'll help you find the mice and then
we'll—"

"We can't find them," he said flatly. "I've been asking every kid at the park. The cub scouts at St. Jude's
had a paper drive, and I got a list of them and I went
to every house and asked them if they got our mice.
But nobody knew nothing about them."

So that's why he had set off every morning on his bicycle, and come back silent and discouraged.

"Brian, one of the little boys called the other one Duffy. I remembered last night. He asked the one that was pulling the wagon, 'Will your dad let you keep them, Duffy?' "

She had hoped his set face would lighten. It didn't. "I don't know anybody named Duffy. Once I did, but he moved away a long time ago."

"And this Duffy kid said something about his father sleeping in the daytime. And I've been remembering that he didn't say a word about his mother. I mean, you'd have thought the other boy would have said, 'Will your mother let you keep them?' Maybe he hasn't got one. Do you know anyone that hasn't got a mother?"

With the morning sun in his face, Brian seemed to turn that over in his mind. And then his eyes did turn to her wonderingly, hopefully. "Could that kid have said 'Dubby' instead of 'Duffy'? Because there's a kid they call Dubby—I guess cause his last name is something like that."

"Yes, it could have been Dubby."

"This Dubby kid don't go to St. Jude's. I see him once in a while in the park. Yeh, once some kid told me he didn't have a mother."

"Then we ought to be able to find him. Come on

with me, Brian. We'll scour all of South Denver, and we'll get the mice back before the twins get home."

Brian got to his feet with alacrity. Like a knight going into action, he thrust the sword through the leather loop he had fastened to his belt. "I know a fellow named Osbo that traded Dubby for a glove once. I bet he'll know where he lives."

ELEVEN

At the edge of town Katie Rose parked the Triumph outside a small cafe, and she and Brian went in for milk and doughnuts. She telephoned home. Although it was eight o'clock now, Ben was still waiting for news. Yes, she had found Brian. "But tell Liz and Stacy not to look for us for a while. We're going to hunt up a boy named Dubby."

Locating a little boy at nine o'clock on a Thursday morning took some doing. Brian directed Katie Rose to a small park on the east side of the university. Not many boys had congregated there yet. Osbo was not about, and the ones they queried were very vague about Dubby's whereabouts or activities. One thought he'd gone some place with his scout troop. Another told them his name was Dubberly. No one knew where he lived.

Their next stop was at a drugstore and a telephone directory. Two Dubberlys were listed in it but both addresses, Katie Rose realized, were far, far away, and not at all within wagon-pulling distance of Hubbell Street.

Brian said, "If it *is* Dubby, I saw him once at Pearl's bakery. Maybe she'd know where he lives."

Katie Rose drove there, and they entered the shop with its delectable smell. They had to wait until Pearl boxed a chocolate cake for a customer and then righted a sign on the counter that said, "Day-old bread. One-third off." Katie Rose explained why they were searching for a boy called Dubby.

Yes, Pearl knew him, and yes, his name was Dubberly. The reason it wasn't in the phone book was because Dubberly, senior, was a typesetter and worked late and didn't want the phone waking him in the morning.

"Does Dubby have a mother?" Katie Rose asked.

Leave it to Pearl to know all there was to know. She shook her head. "The Mrs. took a flyer about four years ago. And good riddance, if you ask me. And if you ask me, Dubby senior won't be crazy about being routed out of bed before noon after working late—"

"We can't wait till noon," Brian said.

"Okay, come out here, and I'll show you where he lives." On the sidewalk, she pointed down the Boulevard. "Go past the traffic light two blocks, and then turn right. You'll see a yellow stucco apartment house on the next corner. A little old and beat-up—but that's it."

They found the apartment house. Brian's only comment as they entered the small and stuffy vestibule was, "I hope Dubby's home."

"So do I," Katie Rose echoed, as she studied the list of tenants and pressed the button beside the name plate, J. DUBBERLY.

She pressed it again and again before she heard a click and then a man's voice demanding, "Yeh? Who is it?"

"Is Dubby—your little boy—home?"

"No. Left early this morning. Camp-out, they call it. What do you want?"

"Did he bring home some white mice about two weeks ago?"

"Who is this anyway? If this is the management, I told you—"

"No, I'm the girl that gave the mice to him. We'd like them back. I—we'll even pay Dubby because we have to have them—"

The irritable, raspy voice interrupted, "Who said anything about pay? I was glad enough to get rid of them. That fool kid should've known that when you live in an apartment house—"

"You mean you don't have them now?"

The voice was louder and somehow defensive. "Look, I try to do right by the boy—God knows I do. But mice in that smelly igloo! So when I found someone who'd take them off our hands, I just figured—" A giant yawn muffled his voice.

"Who did you—I mean, who took them off your hands?"

"Who are you anyway? And if you gave the mice away, what do you want them back for?"

"I'm Katie Rose Belford. We live down on Hubbell Street." And she confessed to Dubby's father, who was only a sleepy disgruntled voice coming through a speaker, how she had hurriedly disposed of the mice when their owners were away—

"Tell him about the fishhook stuck in Matt's cheek," Brian prompted beside her.

"What's that? What's that about a fishhook?" the voice wanted to know.

Katie Rose explained that too, and about the trade for a cage of copper wire. "And so we've just got to get the mice back before the twins come home this evening."

"I gave them to a girl named Linda Daniels. She's taking some course at school"—another drawn-out yawn—"and she wanted to try out their reflexes or some such fool thing. Wait till I get my glasses and I'll tell you where she lives." Silence, and then the voice over the speaker gave an address in Harmony Heights. "That's it. So you argue it out with her. I hope you get them back all right."

"Thanks, Mr. Dubberly."

Again they climbed into Miguel's low car. Katie Rose turned it toward Harmony Heights. "One more stop and the mice are ours," she assured Brian, who sat tense in the bucket seat beside her. "Because this girl would just as soon have any other white mice for whatever experiments she wants to try."

They stopped in front of a low ranch house of red brick with white window boxes, aflame with flowers. A woman in a summery dress, a headpiece of flowers and veil, and clutching white gloves and purse was standing on the porch as though she were waiting to be called for in a car. A big yellow cat was lying on one of the white wicker porch chairs.

Well, at least they'd be conversing with a person in the flesh, instead of a disembodied voice over a speaker. Katie Rose and Brian walked up to the porch steps, and Katie Rose asked the woman if she had a daughter Linda.

Oh yes, but Linda wasn't home. The woman glanced at a car that turned the corner.

"Did she bring home two white mice? Because we'd like them back, and we'll get her two more if she—"

Linda's mother gave a rippling laugh. "Honestly, those mice. And that girl. She's always starting something, and leaving it to someone else to finish. She brings home the mice with all her big talk of training them to know that when she rings a bell, she'll feed them. She read something about it in a book. And then she gets a chance to be counsellor at a summer camp, and off she goes, big as life, and leaves the drawer of dirt and mice. I told her when she brought them home that you couldn't have mice and Topaz in the same house." She indicated the sleeping yellow cat.

Brian's anxious voice asked, "Haven't you got them now?"

"Land no, child. I just said to my husband that I had enough on my mind without having to worry—"

"What did you do with them?" Katie Rose asked fearfully.

"We have the nicest truck-farmer that always brings in black dirt for my roses every spring, and my husband likes his tomato plants better than—"

"Did you give them to him?" Katie Rose broke in. "What is his name?"

"Oh land of love, what *is* his name? It's a big long foreign-sounding one—"

"Can't you remember?" Brian begged. "Because we've got to get the mice back before Matt and Jill come home."

The flustered woman looked at his imploring face. "I gave him a check. Now wait—just wait and I'll see—because that's one thing my husband rakes me over the coals about if I don't put down the name of every check on the stub—"

She opened her purse, pawed through its assorted contents for her checkbook. She found it and thumbed through it, talking all the while and glancing up at every sound of a car, while Katie Rose and Brian stood in nervous suspense.

A car drew up at the curb and a woman, also dressed and hatted for a summer luncheon party, called out, "Come on, Amy—we still have to pick up Nancy."

"Oh dear, I've got to go—we're late now. If you'd come back this evening—"

She was starting to close her checkbook when Katie Rose, looking over her shoulder, said, "There! There's a big long name. Maybe that's it."

"Yes, that's it. Manzanares. V. Manzanares—and I'm sure he said his first name was Vincent, but I could see I wouldn't have room to write that. And he lives out near Derby." She was halfway to the car, but she halted to say, "You can find his name in the phone book because you know after that hail the first part of June we phoned him for more tomato plants." She even called out from the car, "It's on *something Road*."

Katie Rose and Brian walked slowly toward their car, slowly climbed in, muttering, "V. Manzanares— V. Manzanares," so they wouldn't forget. Katie Rose said, "Brian, Jeanie only lives a few blocks from here. Thursday—she won't be working at the clinic. Let's go there and look in her phone book, and maybe she or her mother will know how to get there. O.K.?"

He nodded.

It was cheering to walk through the Kincaid pink door. Jeanie was home and so was her mother. They listened sympathetically to the saga of the disappearing, the hard-to-track-down mice. They were helpful, too. Jeanie ran her finger down the list of Manzanareses in the phone book, and said triumphantly, "Here we are! V. Manzanares, 7105 Pinhorn Road."

Mrs. Kincaid said, "Katie Rose, you went out to that new Maplewood Mart. It's in that general area. And you remember, Jeanie, last fall when we drove out near Derby to buy tomatoes for ketchup." She found a city map and showed Katie Rose the best way to go.

It was noon by now, and Jeanie set out Cokes and made sandwiches. Brian wouldn't sit down. "We ought to go, Katie Rose," he urged every minute or two.

"Why don't you go with them, Jeanie, and help Katie Rose find Pinhorn Road?" her mother suggested.

"That I will," Jeanie agreed. "Wait till I get my dark glasses—haven't you got a pair, Katie Rose? I'll find you one. We'll storm the Manzanares' truck farm and rescue the mice."

She sat in the bucket seat beside Katie Rose. In the space for luggage behind, Brian sat leaning forward as though in that posture he could push the car faster. It was a long drive out Derby way with the hot sun beating down, and the dry wind blowing their hair across cheeks and sunglasses. They drove almost to the Maplewood Mart, and then veered north.

They stopped at a filling station, not only for gas, but for directions. Brian was studying the sign on the building next to it that read, LITTLE SHOE TAVERN.

"Why do you suppose they call it Little Shoe?" he asked.

"That's the name of a creek out here," Jeanie said.

They had to stop again to ask a woman working in her garden where Pinhorn Road was. After finding it, Katie Rose drove the wrong way on it for a mile or so before they realized it. She had to find a wide spot in the road before she could maneuver the little car around and backtrack.

The houses here in this rural district weren't num-
bered, though some of the mailboxes on posts close
to the road were. Some of them bore names. At length,
Brian called out, "There it is. See?" and he pointed
to an aluminum box with MANZANARES rudely painted
on it.

Katie Rose pulled the car off the road. They went
through a gate into the small acreage consisting of a
yellowish frame house surrounded by many low sheds
and garden patches.

A big, brawny boy of perhaps eighteen left off his
hoeing of what Katie Rose thought were cabbage plants
to watch their approach. A great shock of black hair
reached low over his bold, black and unfriendly eyes.

Katie Rose said, "We're looking for V. Manzanares."

"That's my old man. He ain't home. I'm Pete. I'm
the only one here." He wasted no smile on them.

"Does he still have the mice that Mrs. Daniels gave
him?"

"*He* ain't got 'em. He gave 'em to me," he said
shortly. He motioned toward a nearby shed. "I got
'em in there." He hunkered down to adjust a hose
nozzle so the water would run down a furrow of the
young plants he had been hoeing.

Brian hurried into the shed, and the two girls followed uncertainly. After the sun's glare, it took a min-

ute to adjust to the shed's dimness. It smelled of damp earth and fertilizer, and was cluttered with tools and boxes of dirt.

But there was the drawer of dirt and the Quonset-shaped screen top with the makeshift door held in place by the fence staple and safety pin. There was the same Mason jar top for water—though it was dry now. Somewhere in its travels, the cracked saucer from the dump had been replaced by a red plastic one.

Brian pushed up close to the cage and gave a low chirp-chirp, and out of the dirt came the two small white inhabitants. "They know me," he breathed triumphantly. "After all this time, they still know me."

With that, young Manzanares entered with a loud clunk of hoe and came up to the cage. A darting streak of white, and the mice were instantly out of sight in an underground tunnel of their own making.

"They're afraid of you," Brian said.

Pete Manzanares gave a mean chuckle. "I don't give a damn whether they are or not."

Jeanie looked at Katie Rose. She had the ability to say a whole sentence in one look, and this time her look said, "Did you ever see such a surly lout?" Katie Rose's quirk of lips answered Jeanie's unspoken comment.

But she said as diplomatically as she could, "The

mice belong to Brian here, and his brother and sister. I was the one who gave them away. But now Matt and Jill are coming back—"

Brian's pleading voice added, "Matt got a fishhook in his cheek, and he traded for a new cage to put them in."

Pete's sullen eyes showed no flicker of friendliness, much less of sympathy. "They're my mice now," he said.

"But we've just got to get them back," Katie Rose persisted. "I'd be willing to pay you—something—for them."

His eyes measured all three of them, and then glanced out to the Triumph parked at the gate. A greedy gleam came into his black eyes. "How much?"

Jeanie flung out, "You've got a lot of nerve. They don't belong to you. You've only had them a few days."

He turned his dour, ungiving gaze on her. "Ten days," he corrected. "My old man brought 'em home and gave 'em to me." He was still holding the hoe, and he leaned on it now to impart, "I know of a fellow—a sort of scientific bird—and he raises snakes to make venom. And, like I hear, he'll pay good for mice to feed his snakes so they'll give more venom."

A strangled cry came from Brian. "Oh no! Not Gertie and George—not to feed snakes."

The boy went on, unmoved, "And, like I hear, he'll pay five bucks for a pair of mice 'cause he's runnin' low on 'em."

"You're lying," Jeanie accused him. "He can get all the mice he wants—and not for five bucks a pair."

Some instinct made Katie Rose nudge her to keep quiet. Nothing could be gained by making this heartless—yes, and greedy fellow more inimical. Conscious of Brian's white tortured face, she was thinking fast. She remembered that when she had stopped for gas on the way out, she'd had three one-dollar bills in her billfold. Pete would surely take that much and let them have the cage and mice. It was highway robbery, but what was money compared to Brian's suffering?

She took out the three dollars. "This is all I've got, but I'll give you these—"

His grimy paw shot out and snatched the bills out of her hand before she could finish the sentence. "That's fine," he said. "Now when you bring the other two, the mice are all yours."

There was shocked silence in the cluttered shed. Jeanie's fist clenched, but again Katie Rose nudged her to silence. This situation was too desperate for name-calling, no matter how justifiable. This situation called for—

She looked at Brian standing so close to the cage his head almost touched the safety pin fastening. She had a flash of inspiration. She drew a long breath, swallowing down her indignation and fury. She turned to the stocky Pete and gave him her most winning smile. She said on a gay, admiring laugh, "You'll be a big business tycoon one of these days, Pete. You've got a right to charge us whatever you can get from someone else. I guess I can scurry up another two dollars if I have to."

He melted a very little. "How far away do you live?"

"Miles and miles. And the sun is *so* hot and we got *so* thirsty coming out." She laughed archly this time. "And now that you've taken all our money, we can't even stop for a cold drink. So could we get a drink before we start back?"

Yes, he was a shade less belligerent. "Can you drink out of a hose? The house is shut up because the old lady sprayed for miller moths before she went over to that new store."

Jeanie had listened to all this in wide-eyed amazement until Katie Rose gave her a cautious wink. Jeanie flashed back a look that said, "Whatever you're up to, I'll carry along." She added eagerly, "Heavens, I'm so thirsty I could drink out of a fire hose."

"Come on then," the boy said and started for the door.

Yes, Jeanie had caught on. As she followed Pete,

she stumbled over the door sill and laughed loudly at her awkwardness. Brian, deep in his misery, still stood in front of the cage where the mice hadn't shown so much as a whisker after their first delving into the dirt. Under cover of Jeanie's scrambling and laughter, Katie Rose said in a vehement whisper as she passed him, "*Get* the mice."

Pete Manzanares hadn't manners enough to turn the pressure lower on the hose. But that was all right. It gave the girls more chance to shriek as the water sprayed their faces— "Whoops! I got more in my eye than I did in my mouth."

Katie Rose even showed a great interest in Pete's rows of cabbage plants. "Kohlrabi," he corrected, and she and Jeanie laughed hilariously. As though nothing in the world was so funny as to mistake cabbage plants for kohlrabi.

Brian emerged from the shed and started toward the car. He said only, "I don't want a drink. We better be going, Katie Rose." She decided, not from his poker face but by the hands in his pockets, that they had indeed better be going.

"Thanks, Pete—thanks a lot for the drink."

"You won't forget? Two bucks more and you can take the mice."

She and Jeanie both called back, "Don't worry. We won't forget."

Brian commented as they reached the car, "It was Gertie I had trouble with. I fastened the door back just the way it was."

They drove down Pinhorn Road chortling happily. Now they could call Pete all the names they had longed to call him to his face. "Glutton! Sadist!" Katie Rose ended.

"Then my chirping them out and reaching in and getting them wasn't stealing, was it?" Brian asked.

"Stealing, my eye!" Jeanie exploded. "Not when he did Katie Rose out of her three bucks."

The dirt road was winding and narrow, and Katie Rose wasn't sure of the turn to take to get off it. A car was coming toward them, and she pulled off to the side and stopped, planning to ask the driver for directions. But when the uncoming car was almost to them, it turned off and stopped beside a white house at the side of the road.

The car was a two-tone job of chocolate brown and faded pink—yes, and with both visible fenders badly rumpled.

"Jeanie, I wish you'd look!"

But Jeanie was already staring at the car and the small woman who flippantly stepped out of it. And at the man who got out on the other side and came around to take her arm. He was dressed in the gray denim of a garage worker or filling station attendant. Neither one of them so much as glanced at the little car so near at hand that its occupants could see the splashy flowers in the woman's dress, and the intimate way the man pulled her close. They could even hear him laugh, and see her coy toss of blond hair.

"Veddy, veddy cozy," Jeanie said on a harsh laugh.

Katie Rose mused, "So this is where our pansy-thrower lives. Well, that figures—for her to be out here in the same neck of the woods as Maplewood Mart."

Brian was pointing toward the next corner and saying, "Right here's where we turn. Don't you remember it was by the house with the white wagon wheels in the front yard? Go on, Katie Rose. We'd better get home before Matt and Jill come."

"Go on," Jeanie echoed. "The very sight of that woman gives me the creeps."

TWELVE

"Saved by the bell," Katie Rose murmured to Jeanie as she stopped the Triumph at the side of the Belford house. For there was no sign of a Bannon pickup *or* the twins.

It was late afternoon. The Chevy was already parked, which meant that Ben was home from work. Stacy and Liz came hurrying to the gate. "Mission accomplished," Jeanie chuckled, with a nod toward Brian who was making for the back door and saying over his shoulder, "It's pretty hot for them in my pocket."

Katie Rose walked on stiff and weary legs into the

kitchen. She had strength only to wash her hands at the sink before she dropped down at the dinette table. Liz said, "You look fagged out for fair, childeen. Now you, Stacy, don't be asking questions till the girls have had a sip of tea." She filled their cups, and asked Katie Rose, "Maybe you'd like lemon in it?"

She shook her head. And this thought passed through her tired mind: It was one thing for the housekeeper at the Belford mansion to give time to all those fancy touches of cloves stuck in lemon slices, and open-faced sandwiches. But she didn't have to give a long day to scouring half the state for a runaway boy, and given-away mice.

Brian had time only to transpose Gertie and George to a shoe box, when the back door was thumped open and in came Jill and Matt. Jill clutched a rattly sack which turned out to hold odds and ends from the Bannon junk yard. Matt carried the bell-shaped, copper cage that had cost him so dear. A bandage covered a good part of his face, and over it his darkened and swollen eye showed.

No one kissed them in greeting because the twins didn't like "slobberin' over."

Jill's first words were, "Is Ben home yet?"

"He's taking a shower," Stacy said.

"I suppose he'll give us Hail Columbia."

"You didn't expect a Purple Heart, did you?"

Jill hastily changed the subject. "You ought to see all the beards everybody's got in Bannon. So they'll look old-timey for Cherry Day. Wait'll you see Grandda."

Grandda came in on that remark, carrying the twins' luggage. "No remarks about my alfalfa crop," he said, fingering the growth of bristly red hair on his chin.

Katie Rose asked, "Is Aunt Kitty still so hot under the collar?"

He grinned. "Not quite. Not since the dentist told her the tooth Jill knocked loose on her one wouldn't have to come out."

"Oh indeed, Kitty!" Liz discounted in a mutter.

Jill's mutter was, "I just barely touched him."

Grandda hadn't time to stop for tea. He had to get back to Bannon for a Cherry Day committee meeting. "Don't forget the last Saturday in July," he said from the doorway.

"We'll be there," Stacy said. "If you're driving the stagecoach, be sure and save room for us in it."

"We'll find room for all of you in the parade," he promised. "And, Jeanie, you come too."

"I'd love to, Mr. O'Byrne."

As the door closed behind him, Liz said, "I wonder now that he didn't bring in eggs and some of the cream that must be piling up on him."

Katie Rose didn't wonder. Again she squirmed in unhappy remembrance.

Ben, barefooted, emerged from the shower in his faded and frayed robe. The culprits said in unison, "We didn't start the fight—honest, we didn't, Ben."

"Oh no, you never start anything. You're always the innocent victims."

"It was Kitty's one," insisted Jill, "and he nearly put Matt's eye out. That's what I told them—that another half-inch and Matt'd been blind in one eye all his life, and it'd all been his fault. And Matt *could* have got lockjaw and starved to death, and it'd've been his own fault too—that's what I told them."

"I'll bet you told them," Ben said. "I'll bet you told yourself and Matt right out of Bannon."

The two backed against the sink and waited with lowered eyes and shuffling feet for Ben's tirade. It didn't come. Instead, he pulled Matt to him and looked closely at the dressing. He asked what the doctor said about changing the bandage.

"Does it hurt, kid?" he asked.

"Naw, not much."

"Brian's sleeping in my room," Ben said, "because Katie Rose rented yours to a fellow named Perry Mc-Harg. But you can sleep in your own top bunk, Matt."

Jill gasped out, "Where am I going to sleep?"

She looked so woebegone, so unwanted, that Katie

Rose put her arm around her. "With me, honey."

"In your room?" Her aghast voice was saying that this separating of the three inseparables was greater punishment than she had even anticipated. "Do you want me to?" she asked bluntly.

Another time Katie Rose might have answered honestly, "No, I don't," for it had been heaven to have a room to herself. And Jill, tomboyish, noisy, and contrary, would be worse than Stacy. But the day had been a shaking-up one for Katie Rose; she felt older, and somehow more *motherly* toward the littles. She patted Jill on the cheek. "Of course I do. We'll clean out a drawer in the dresser for your things."

Liz said gently, "Get along now, you littles, and wash up and come on down for tea."

It wasn't Katie Rose but Stacy who enjoined, "And use the red towels. They're yours, and you're not to touch the others."

Jeanie handed Ben a cup of tea, and said impulsively, "Oh, Ben, I like you. You're swell."

Stacy had a baby-sitting job that evening. It was with a spoiled and demanding boy of ten whom she called Prince Charlie. "Only to get enough money for my white swimsuit and petaled cap would I put up with the pampered prince for an evening," she said. "Him and his allegories!"

She meant *allergies,* but Katie Rose was too tired to

correct her. Ben drove Jeanie home, and dropped Stacy off *en route*. The littles hurriedly drank their tea, stuffed down three slices of bread and jelly apiece, and then Katie Rose heard the great scurrying, arguing, and pounding upstairs.

She was still slumped at the dinette table when Liz answered the phone. It was Ben calling, she reported, to say that the Kincaids had asked him to stay for an outdoor supper. Liz added, "Stretch out there and rest, Mavourneen, while I ready up a bit here. You've been on the go since early dawn."

"Maybe I will—just for a minute."

The dinette bench was wide and long, and covered with a leatherette cushion. And Katie Rose was suddenly heavy-eyed. Yes, just for a minute, she told herself, and then she must see about dinner—because—she had—a—boarder—

She wakened with a start and sat up. It was dusk, and someone was rattling things out of a sack. Perry McHarg smiled into her sleep-fogged eyes. "Katie Rose, you're a sweetheart. You've had quite a day of it rescuing the mice, from what I heard Brian telling the twins."

"Brian? Telling Matt and Jill? But when we were driving back from Pinhorn Road, Brian said—or we both decided—not to tell the twins the mice had ever left home."

He laughed. "I guess it was too good for him to keep. Especially your outsmarting some bozo who was about to drop the squirming little mice into a snake's mouth. So Liz and I decided you weren't to stir a hand for dinner." He was busily unwrapping packages. "We're having hamburgers and potato salad."

She laughed too in wondrous relief and content. At that moment Perry McHarg was one of them, not a watchful-eyed critic. Even as Jeanie, she said impulsively, "Perry, I like you. You're swell."

"You're more than swell. Push the hair out of your eyes, and how do you like your hamburger?"

The littles had returned the first day of July. Now there were eight instead of six at the dining table. Now Katie Rose doubled Mrs. McHarg's recipes. That is, she doubled them for a day, and then she doubled them, plus a half. She realized that the two little McHarg girls didn't eat as much as *one* of the Belford littles. Next she trebled the recipes.

Jill was far from an amenable roommate. The first night she pulled out of the suitcase and put on a rumpled pajama bottom which reeked of some cleaner she and Matt had used to shine up the copper cage. The next night when she looked for it, Katie Rose said, "I put it to soak in the washer. Here's something you can sleep in."

The something was an outgrown pair of her own baby-doll pajamas. Jill took the ruffly two pieces between her fingers with a look of horror. "But these're for a girl."

"What do you think you are?" Katie Rose countered.

"I'll just wear them for this one night," Jill compromised.

She wore them for more than one night. Katie Rose told her the pajama half had fallen apart in washing.

On Saturday afternoon Katie Rose was sitting on her bed writing to Miguel in Washington. She was putting on paper, "Guess what? Jeanie and I saw the woman who threw the box of pansies at your camera. She lives out on Pinhorn Road—" when Jill burst into the room.

She flung herself onto the bench of the vanity with such force that its slim curved legs creaked in protest. "Ben wouldn't take *me*. And look—just look at how long it is." Jill pulled a swath of her light brown hair out to its full length.

So that was it! Ben, home from work early, had taken Matt and Brian to the barbershop for a haircut. Heretofore, Jill had been the third to get a short boy-cut.

"Did *you* tell him not to?" Jill accused.

"I did *not*. Ben thought your hair would look prettier if you let it grow out a little. It would, too. I noticed a girl in church Sunday with hair like yours, only she had it combed back, and it was shiny gold from brushing—"

"Brushing? Who wants to brush hair?" She got up and flounced herself out with this final accusation, "You're just trying to make a sissy out of me."

It would take a lot of trying, Katie Rose thought.

During the school year, Jill wore the St. Jude uniform of plaid jumper, white blouse, and green blazer. But it was shucked off, and she was in shirt and Levi's two minutes after she came in the door. It was the same with the white blouse and blue denim wraparound skirt she wore to church on Sunday.

"If only, by some miracle," Mother had often sighed, "we could get her into a *pretty* dress."

Jill bellowed now from the foot of the stairs, "I'm going up to Downey's Drug to see if there are any deliveries."

Ben had told the littles that first morning after the twins returned from Bannon, "You're not to ask Katie Rose for spending money. She needs what she has for groceries. You hustle up some lawn-cutting jobs."

And so they had, besides making deliveries for Downey's Drug and gloating over every tip they got. "Men always give us more than women," Brian told Katie Rose.

Monday was the Fourth of July. The Belfords had decided to picnic in the park, for there was to be a swimming and diving meet at the lake, with Bruce Seerie one of the contestants. Ben would go after Jeanie in the Chevy, and Perry McHarg offered to take the others in his station wagon.

This Saturday afternoon when Katie Rose finished Miguel's letter, she drove to the supermarket to buy the picnic food. Ben had paid his ten dollars when he returned from work, and Liz gave her another ten.

She jostled her way through the maze of shoppers who were buying for the two-day holiday, and filled her basket with barbecued chickens, potato chips, pickles, paper plates and cups. And a kidney-shaped can of ham that cost four dollars and forty-seven cents. Five cents a pound didn't seem much for watermelon. But the checker put it on the scales and rang up a dollar and eighty-five cents.

Goodness, how that cash register did total up! Katie Rose went home with very little of the twenty dollars she had come with.

They were in the crowded park on the evening of the Fourth. Katie Rose was gathering up a few remnants of the picnic while they all discussed whether they should stay on for the fireworks after dark, and Stacy was watching for Bruce to join them, when a small boy and bicycle suddenly appeared at Katie Rose's elbow.

"Here!" He was handing her the small thin envelope theater tickets came in. "Dad said for me to give them to you, and I went to your house, and the old man next door said you were all over here at the park."

She had to stare at the towheaded boy for a moment, before she said, "You're Dubby that I gave the mice to."

He nodded and, all in one breath, explained that his father did printing—programs, he guessed—for the theater at Acacia Gardens, and they'd given him two passes for the show, but he said to tell her he wasn't much for night life and he thought maybe she and her beau could use them. He added as an afterthought, "He felt kinda bad because he didn't have the mice when you wanted them back, and then he felt bad when he called that girl he gave them to and her mother said—"

"You tell him we got them back."

"The tickets are for tonight," he volunteered, and broke into her thanks to say, "Dad says when we get us a house, I can have mice of my very own." On that, he and his bicycle were lost in the crowd.

Katie Rose took out and fingered the magic bits of cardboard. They were for tonight, and the show at

Acacia Gardens was *The Sound of Music*. It was like a windfall from heaven, or rather from a disembodied and irritated voice she had heard only over a speaker.

Everyone was talking at once. Perry McHarg said, "Please say I'm your beau, Katie Rose, so I can take you," and Jeanie was saying, "You'll love it, Katie Rose. We saw it Wednesday night."

Jeanie's parents, who were theater lovers, had season tickets for Acacia Gardens.

And that's how it happened that, an hour later, Katie Rose came down the Belford stairs in her fashion-show outfit, her eyes purple as her necklace with excited anticipation. For this joyous occasion she was wearing her Prom Night wrap. The very soft luxury of its satin and fuzzy *almost* fur added an extra lift to her spirits. So did the admiring light in Perry's eyes when he opened the car door for her.

She sat beside him in the station wagon while he took the long drive from South Denver to the amusement park on the north side.

"The Park of Beauty," Acacia Gardens advertised itself, and it was true. Hanging lanterns and flower baskets overhead. The smell of caramel popcorn. The lilting melody from the merry-go-round vying with music from the dance pavilion next to the theater; and both drowned out by the roar of the roller coasters and the screams of their riders.

Theater and music had always spelled enchantment for Katie Rose. She sat beside Perry soaking up the music, quite forgetful of the way money and food disappeared in the Belford home. Once when she was stirred by a song and needed a hand to grope for, his hand was there. He squeezed hard and said again, "You're sweet, Katie Rose."

Albums of *The Sound of Music* were on sale in the lobby. Perry bought Katie Rose one. "It's that song, 'I am Sixteen, Going on Seventeen,' that's my special present to you," he told her when they were dancing in the pavilion after the show.

"But I'm an older sixteen, going on seventeen than that girl in the play," she said.

He gave her a quizzical look. "In some ways," he conceded.

So was dancing enchantment. The purple pumps pinched her feet, but she didn't feel it. She sang to the music.

Perry McHarg said, "Your press agents were right that first evening at the McHargs' when they said you could sing and dance better than anyone in the whole world."

He meant the braggart little McHarg girls.

Many of the Adams High students were at Acacia Gardens that night and dancing in the pavilion. Katie Rose couldn't help preening herself to be seen with a boy who was unmistakably "college"—not high-school.

Her enchanted evening. They were dancing the last dance when he said rather soberly, "You know, Katie Rose, there's something I've been wanting to say to you—" His eyes rested on her flushed cheeks and shining eyes, and he added, "But no, this doesn't seem the right time, or the right place."

The music stopped. She almost said, "Go ahead and say it." Why wasn't any time or any place right for a boy to tell a girl she was very special to him? Maybe he wanted to tell her that she had been from that first night at the McHargs', and that was why he had phoned to ask if they had an extra room—

He tucked the furry Prom Night wrap about her. "The musicians are putting their instruments to bed. It's time to go. But first I'll buy you some cotton candy."

THIRTEEN

Where did the money go?

That week and the next Ben gave Katie Rose his ten dollars on Saturday when he came home from work. Liz added hers to it. Katie Rose, her shopping list ready, would lose no time in taking off for the shopping center in the Triumph. But the refrigerator and cupboards would be practically bare by the time Perry McHarg paid her his board money Tuesday evening.

That lone twenty-dollar bill, the last of her backlog, was long since gone.

Not only did those four sandwiches in Ben's lunch

decimate a loaf of bread, but he said, "Katie Rose, if you don't mind, skip all that fancy sandwich spread, and use ham or cheese." A few days later he suggested, "Could you put in doughnuts or apple tarts instead of those thin little cookies?"

He meant the slice'n bake ones she bought in rolls.

She could slice and bake two of the rolls (forty-nine cents each) and they went like chaff in the wind. Now you see them—now you don't!

It was the same with her fruit centerpiece on the sideboard. She never saw the fruit go, but by night there would be maybe one greenish peach and two plums, and her bunch of grapes would be only a skeleton of twigs. When she scolded about it, the littles would regard her with wide, innocent eyes and mutterings of, "Well gee, I just took a couple of grapes as I went by." Or Stacy would say, "I grabbed off a peach or two for Bruce and me." Or maybe Ben would sing out, "I killed Cock Robin. I ate a banana before I went to bed. I didn't know it was a Federal offense."

Her beautiful fruit picture had to go.

It was such a hungry crew that gathered about the Belford table. Matt, the embattled warrior, now wore a smaller bandage under his discolored eye. His appetite had never been impaired. Katie Rose had forgotten the rapidity with which the littles could clean up their first plateful, and then look around for more.

Ben's days on the cement gang seemed to give him hollow legs. *Three* eggs for breakfast! Stacy fretted about the soreness of her sunburned shoulders even while she reached deep into the icebox for a snack. Liz's capacity was in keeping with her bulk. Even the boarder was not what you'd call a light eater.

But Katie Rose stubbornly adhered to McHarg menus.

When Mother served soup, she dipped a cup into the pot of broth thick with vegetables, rice, and barley (and made rich by those backbones from Wetzel's). Yet Mrs. McHarg always said, "I wonder that anyone makes soup these days when you can buy delicious mixes that only take a few minutes."

Thirty-nine cents for a box with two packs. It said right on the box that each pack served four. Mathematically then, two packs would serve eight. They didn't. Neither did three, because Ben or Stacy would be sure to get up from the table and ask, "who wants more soup?" And Katie Rose would have to admit, "That's all of it."

Even for a first course it took four packs of soup mix.

When mother cooked green beans she put on a big kettle of fresh ones, seasoned with strips of bacon (off the slab from Bannon). The McHarg menus called for frozen ones, seasoned with slivered almonds browned in butter. The McHarg recipes leaned heavily on those slivered almonds, as well as mushrooms, canned bouillon, sour and whipping cream.

For four people, Mrs. McHarg used half the package of a dozen brown'n serve rolls. Katie Rose tried *twicing* it. Hah! Now she was serving two dozen. You'd think three rolls apiece would be ample—but there was never a crumb left.

On Thursday morning of the second week following the picnic and the enchanted evening at Acacia Gardens, Stacy asked, "Are you in a good mood this morning, my beautiful sybil?"

Katie Rose laughed. "You mean *sibling*. Yes, fair to middlin'."

But her mood had been more fair than middlin' since her evening of music and dancing with Perry McHarg. Nothing gave a girl that inner glow like knowing that a man is just waiting for a chance to tell her how much she means to him. Often, feeling his thoughtful eyes on her, she was sure he was on the verge of telling her.

Stacy's interest in Katie Rose's spirits had to do with her borrowing the fashion-show dress. "The Seeries asked me to the birthday dinner for Bruce tonight. And I long to wow them. Now, Katie Rose, you can wear my new swimsuit and the petaled cap whenever your little heart desires."

Her heart did desire for Perry to see her in it. That night at the Coach and Four he had said, "We'll come here for a swim and lunch sometime." She was sure he would have taken her before this, but he was giving all his time to gathering data for a paper he was writing for his Marketing class.

Where *did* the money go?

In mid-July Mother's letter to Katie Rose enclosed a twenty-dollar bill. "I've got more than I need," she wrote, "because the kinfolks here won't let me spend money for anything. Gran says she hopes Grandda brings you in all the fryers she left. We can't plan yet on coming home, but you tell him whenever you run short of bacon, butter, eggs, or such."

Oh dear, if Mother only knew she couldn't turn to Grandda!

Most of the twenty went for bacon, butter, eggs, and such. The Belfords weren't used to skimping on those items, so that five pounds of butter, five of bacon, and five dozen eggs fairly melted away.

Where did the money *go?*

On the third Tuesday in July when Perry McHarg paid her his board money, she had to hurry to Pearl's Bakery for bread for dinner, and for lady fingers to use as underpinning for her instant custard.

Pearl, in her friend-of-the-family way, offered her a

jelly roll that had cracked open in the process of rolling. Again Katie Rose took her stand. She told Pearl that she was following planned menus, and couldn't use imperfect or unsaleable items.

Pearl gave her a dumfounded look. She shrugged and said with asperity, "It's all right with me, toots. There are plenty that are glad to get them. I like to help you folks because your mother—and the *rest* of the family—do good turns for me. Give a little, take a little, as your mother says."

The next afternoon Katie Rose shopped with Perry McHarg's board money at the supermarket. But on Friday she had to go again and use the few dollars she had left for extras.

She halted her basket at the dairy counter. She was just reaching for some canned biscuits, when a peremptory hand caught her wrist, and an even more peremptory voice said, "No, Katie Rose—no! Not the canned ones."

She turned and looked into Perry McHarg's hazel eyes under their glasses and those straight bars of eyebrows. "What in the world are you doing here?" she asked in surprise.

He too was holding a can of biscuits which he put back, and made a notation in the notebook he held. She could see that he had covered pages with figures and jotted comments.

"I'm making a comparative report on how to get the most out of a food dollar. Look, ten cents a can for ten biscuits. That doesn't sound like much, but it is. You get more biscuits for the money by buying a ready-mix biscuit flour. But you shouldn't do that either. Your best bet is to buy the flour and shortening and mix them up yourself. So put that can back."

She didn't put it back. She felt her hackles rise. She said belittlingly, "I wondered why you were so nosy—why you asked what the spinach soufflé cost."

"I've got that down too." He flipped a page. "Look here." He picked up the small rectangle of spinach soufflé, all ready for the oven in its pan of fluted aluminum foil. "Fifty-nine cents. There aren't more than two eggs in it. A pound of spinach at eight cents would make twice or three times that much. Want to take some home and try it? You're buying all wrong, Katie Rose. You're paying too much for all this mixing and packaging."

The gall, the unmitigated gall of her boarder telling her how to shop and cook. Her voice was frosty, "Thank you for your helpful advice. I'm sure you'll get A-plus on your paper. But I don't need a Den Mother."

"Now don't get on your high horse. I'm just trying to set you right on how to buy for that hungry mob you're cooking for. I've been wanting to tell you ever since I came."

She stood clutching the cold can of biscuits and staring at the young man with the notebook, while those words sank in. "I've been wanting to tell you—" So this was what he wanted to tell her! And she, conceited fool that she was, had supposed it had to do with his feelings for her as a *girl,* not as a grocery shopper.

A humiliated dirge was pounding under her ribs so that she scarcely heard his earnest words, "I was talking to Carol McHarg about my paper. She agreed with me. She said all these ready-mixes, slice'n bake, brown'n serve, icebox-to-oven deals were a boon for career women, or small families like theirs. Her husband could afford a maid, but she doesn't want the bother of one underfoot. She said she'd rather pay for the built-in maid service in what she buys. And that's exactly what she does every time she buys a package of french fries or frozen, deveined shrimp—"

The fury that rose, choking in her throat, was for herself and her silly jumping to conclusions. She screamed at him, "What I buy and what I don't buy is my business. I told Mother I was going to run the house the way I wanted it run—"

"You're running yourself in a hole you can't crawl out of," he shouted back.

Passing shoppers turned to look at these two young

people quarreling with enough heat over the dairy counter to warm its arctic temperature.

He pulled his voice down. "For goshsakes, girl, don't you realize you're running what you might call a small hotel? How long would it stay in business if it didn't buy with an eye on prices? Oh, I know the days of buying out of a barrel are gone, but there are still markets where you can buy in bulk—"

"Don't tell me. I know all about them. I bumped into those sacks of flour and oatmeal that Grandda brought in from the Bannon mills—"

"I knew it," he broke in triumphantly. "I knew your mother could never raise a husky bunch of kids if she didn't buy like that."

"It so happens that I loathe every bit of that. Slabs of bacon from Bannon and cracked, runny eggs. It so happens that I vowed a vow not to take lopsided cupcakes and doughy doughnuts from Pearl at the bakery, or black bananas and soup bones at Wetzel's." Again her voice would carry two aisles over.

So would his. "What's the matter with slab bacon? What's the matter with black bananas? You sound like Miss Idiot of the Year."

Miss Idiot of the Year! So now she had heard the something he had wanted to tell her.

"All right, all right. You don't have to keep on boarding with Miss Idiot of the Year."

"All right, if you want me to leave. Do you want to refund the half a week of advance board I've paid?"

That brought her up with a jolt. If only she had it to refund. If only she could fling it at him and say, "Take it! And I hope I never lay eyes on you again."

He knew she had spent the money. He was gloating over her. And in that moment she hated him as she had never hated anyone. She found herself backing up a step, her fingers tightening on the can of biscuits—

He put a restraining hand on her arm. "I wouldn't look so good with a dent in my head, Katie Rose. Honest, I didn't mean to make you fightin' mad. But I just thought—"

"I don't care what you just thought. I'll tell you what I think—that you're the most conceited, nosy thing on two legs."

End of conversation.

The customers reaching for frozen cheese cake or patty shells had no way of knowing that the girl who reached for *four* cans of biscuits was really picking up the gauntlet that the young man with a notebook full of figures had tossed at her feet.

The cold war was on between landlady and boarder on Hubbell Street.

The following week she poured his breakfast coffee, and served him cheesecake (frozen and thawed) at dinner, feeling that she was nursing a viper in her bosom. She could practically see him computing the cost of Saturday's stroganoff with mushrooms and sour cream. And Sunday's stuffed capon. Old Hawkeye McHarg!

She was grimly dedicated now, not only to modern cookery for her family, but to showing him she could manage her way.

It was nip and tuck. On one of her shopping tours at the supermarket, she passed a counter with cabbages piled high. She remembered her mother's old standby of ham shank, cabbage and potatoes. But *he* might think she was softening. She bought corn soufflé instead.

If only the McHargs hadn't gone to the mountains, she'd have more evenings of baby-sitting to help her over the financial hump. She was thankful when Mrs. Barton, one of her regular customers, said she'd be needing her on Thursday. Katie Rose always stayed with Mrs. Barton's arthritic mother while the Bartons went to their supper and bridge club. The old lady, who liked Katie Rose to call her Eva, also liked Katie Rose to shampoo, tint, and put up her hair. She also liked Katie Rose to listen to her talk of her young and sought-after days.

"Eva-sitting" always meant that as soon as the Bartons left the driveway, the old lady would say with a snort, "Put away that blah-blah, healthful food Millie left for our dinner." She would have Katie Rose phone for Mexican or Chinese dinners, or barbecued spare-ribs from the drive-in on the Boulevard. This evening they decided on Mexican tacos from the Taco Shack.

True to schedule, the shampooing, the changing of Eva's gray hair to chocolate brown, and the putting it up on curlers was accomplished by the time their suppers arrived, and Katie Rose pushed Eva's wheelchair to the table.

Mr. Barton always conscientiously counted the hours Katie Rose had been there, and paid her on the drive home. But every so often Eva herself slipped Katie Rose a five-dollar bill with a "This is just between us, dearie." And when Katie Rose demurred, she'd give her a roguish wink, "Never mind, never mind. I have to keep on the good side of my hairdresser, don't I?"

This evening when Eva took the bill from her purse, Katie Rose did not demur. She was ashamed of the way her greedy fingers closed over it.

Eva said too, "Now, maybe you can use that package of frozen peas and the jellied veal loaf—yes, and that square of sponge cake—Millie left for us. Let her think we cleaned it all up."

Katie Rose was ashamed too of her alacrity in wrapping up the food. But the jellied veal and sponge cake could go in Ben's lunch. The package of frozen peas, plus two more, would make a serving-around for the family *and* the boarder.

Eva's five and Mr. Barton's three went the next day for groceries. That evening Katie Rose triumphantly served a salad of cooked and deveined shrimp in avocado halves. Make a note of that, Perry McHarg!

But Monday her funds were low again.

She thumbed worriedly through those McHarg menus. There was such a predictable sequence about them. For instance, Sunday: Baked Ham (canned); and the week following there would be Asparagus Cosmopolitan to use up ham slices, and another night, Ham Timbales with mushroom sauce. But when Katie Rose baked the contents of that kidney-shaped can of ham, fancied up McHarg style with brown sugar, pineapple slices, and maraschino cherries, there was barely enough left to make sandwiches for Ben the next day.

Katie Rose noted again, "Monday: Fried Chicken," and Mrs. McHarg's "Tuesday: Cold Fried Chicken." But there was never any cold fried chicken at the Belfords'.

The postman's step on the porch interrupted her troubled reverie. He brought a letter from Mother. Katie Rose read it aloud to Liz.

Aunt Nellie had her good days and her bad. But

Aunt Nellie, herself, worried about Mother's staying on and leaving the "childer" at home. They hadn't heard definitely *when* the twice-removed Callanan relative could arrive and take over. But it should be any day. Mother ended with, "All of you be sure and go to Bannon for Cherry Day so Grandda won't miss us so much."

"It's this coming Saturday," said Liz. "A pity they couldn't be home for it."

Cherry Day in Bannon had always been a gala event for the Belfords. The town took that fourth Saturday in July to pay tribute to the red, juicy cherry that was grown in their orchards and canned in their factory. The opening parade represented the present day with its floats and Cherry Queen, but also the early days when pioneers had come by covered wagon or stagecoach to settle in the fertile valley. For it, the menfolks in Bannon grew beards, and the womenfolks hunted up their grandmothers' dresses.

For Cherry Day, Katie Rose and Stacy wore long print dresses made with snug bodices and voluminous skirts. Stacy's green print was sprigged with white flowers; Katie Rose's yellow dimity was dotted with violet nosegays. If Mother were home, she would wear one of the Gay Nineties costumes she wore at Guido's Supper Club.

Katie Rose went up to her room and found Jill sitting on the floor counting her funds, after adding her share of the morning's lawncutting. Katie Rose knelt by the chest under the window, and sorted through it for her and Stacy's early-day costumes.

She cried out, "Oh look, Jill. Remember when I used to wear this dress for Cherry Day?" She held up a white organdy with puffed sleeves and round neckline. On its full short skirt a splash of red cherries was appliquéd. "And here's the red silk bolero that went with it. It was always one of my favorite dresses," she added fondly.

Jill said, "A boy bumped me on my bicycle and dented my fender, and I still haven't got enough to get it straightened. Big slob!"

"I was just about your age when I wore this dress."

"What'd you keep it for? It's way too little for you now."

"I kept it for *you* when you'd be big enough to wear it," Katie Rose said, though it was a slight fib. "Stand up, and let's see. I'll bet it would just fit you now."

"Me!—in a flubdubby dress like that," Jill snorted.

"Stand up, and let's see if you are as tall as I was when I was eleven going on twelve."

Jill reluctantly stood up in her grass-stained Levi's. Katie Rose held the dress up to her. "Yes, siree, it'd be just perfect, Jill. You know how everybody dresses up for Cherry Day. And Grandda will find room in the parade for all of us. Try it on."

"No. Us kids like to ride burros in the parade. Matt and me don't know about going. Aunt Kitty said she never wanted to lay eyes on us again."

"Oh, Aunt Kitty! She's had time to simmer down by now. You know what she always says—that she cooks three extra chickens for the Belfords for the picnic supper."

Katie Rose's thought flicked to the picnic supper in the fair grounds. Neither Gran nor Aunt Kitty would ever hear to the Belfords contributing to it. Gran always scoffed, "Why should you bring food all the way from Denver? Whoever heard of such a thing?"

Katie Rose folded the white, cherry-trimmed dress and put it back in the chest. Stacy's and her dresses she took downstairs to press.

She opened the chest again that evening to hunt for the small poke bonnets she and Stacy wore with them. Strange! The white dress, with its red bolero, wasn't folded as she had left it. Could that cantankerous Jill have decided to try it on after all?

FOURTEEN

Tuesday was the day Katie Rose put the rainbow towels through the washer as soon as her boarder left for his classes in Hotel and Restaurant Management. She came in from hanging them on the line, and grumbled to Liz, "I suppose old Hawk-eye McHarg knows we haven't got a change of colored towels."

"Oh now, sweet, what if he does? He's such a nice young man. He won't be here much longer, will he?"

"He says he'll be finished at school this coming Friday, but that he may stay on a day or two for interviews and checking swimming pools." But *not* to take his landlady swimming in one. Humiliation was like

191

a sour taste in her mouth. Her, and her bright dream of impressing him in Stacy's glamorous white suit!

"A week—maybe less—and there'll be comings and goings," Liz mused. "Your mother and gran will be home by then, I'm sure."

Liz, herself, was planning on going back to Bannon with Grandda when he came in for Gran. She was going today for a final check-up of her blood pressure. She said, "I don't have to be at the doctor's till three. I could mix up a couple of loaves of Irish bread. Sure, I think Ben—laboring as hard as he does—would find it more filling than boughten bread."

And so would the littles, Katie Rose secretly had to admit. But that, too, would be showing the white feather to the critical, all-seeing student who was bent on proving how wrong she was. She had to stick to her guns until he left. Another week—maybe less.

"No, Liz, don't bother."

At noon the postman brought her a letter from Miguel. She ripped it open, feeling a wave of nostalgia for his easy-going, lovable grin. *He* would never snatch—or try to snatch—a can of biscuits out of her hand.

"And what does the boyeen say?" Liz asked.

"He says his father finally got the book revised. And Miguel is going on to New York with him. Oh, and remember I told him about seeing where the

pansy-throwing woman lived? Listen to what he says:
'That woman did damage Pop's camera when she
banged it with the box of dirt. See enclosed bill.' "

The bill was from a Washington camera shop,
"Authorized Repair Service," and was for fourteen
dollars and fifty cents for replacing the finder lens on
a Leica.

The letter went on: "Pop says there's no chance of
my collecting it from this end. But he says if you
drive out toward Derby and pry it out of her, you can
have it. Bear down on her. Tell her it's a legitimate
debt. Good luck, Petunia."

Fourteen dollars and fifty cents! Hope lifted in
Katie Rose. With that she could finish off with her
boarder in a triumphant flourish. And Mother's and
Gran's return would be as soul-rewarding as she
dreamed. In case Perry McHarg's stay overlapped their
return, so much the better.

"Will you be going out to collect it then?" Liz
asked.

"You bet I will."

Katie Rose telephoned Jeanie at the clinic to tell her
of Miguel's offer. "He sent the bill, and I need that
money like a one-legged man needs a crutch. I'm going to drive out there and—"

"I'll go with you," Jeanie broke in promptly.
"When are you going?"

"I'm taking Liz downtown at three—"

"I can get off then. I'm supposed to stay until four, but I'll work through my noon hour." She lowered her voice, "The very thought of that woman gives me goose flesh, but I can't rest till I know *why* she bolts at the sight of me."

At three that afternoon, Katie Rose dropped Liz off at a downtown medical building. She drove on to where Jeanie, waiting on a busy corner, managed to plop herself into the Triumph before it came to a full stop.

After worrying their way through downtown traffic, they again drove in the direction of Maplewood Mart. Again, after stopping only once for directions, they found Pinhorn Road. They followed its devious winding, and were rewarded by locating first the house with the white wagon wheels at the gate, and then the neat rectangle of white house and green roof across the road.

But today no car sat in the lane beside it. The house itself looked closed tight. They knocked at both the front door and the back without an answer. They walked back to the car, disappointed and irresolute. Across the road in the yard behind the wagon-wheel gate, a stout gray-haired woman was cutting the grass.

"Should we wait for her, Jeanie? It oughtn't to be too long. Remember that day we drove past and saw her coming home? What time was it then?"

"It was later in the day than this."

"If we only knew where she works. I should think that dog-food business would have headquarters some place. Maybe if we marched in there—I mean, maybe she'd be ashamed not to pay us with her boss close at hand. Let's see if the woman across the road knows anything about her."

They walked through the wagon-wheel gate into the yard, which showed signs of loving care. The woman, garbed in a man's blue shirt and pink slacks, rested on the handle of the lawn mower, her face a mottled red from her exertions. "Muggy," she said by way of greeting.

Katie Rose said, "We wondered if you could tell us about the woman in the white house across from you. We drove out to see her, but there's no one home."

The neighbor's unsmiling eyes raked over them. "Are you friends of hers?" she asked abruptly.

"No, we just wanted to see her about—about—"

"Some business," Jeanie finished it. "Do you know her name?"

"Not her last name. Sometimes I wonder if she does herself—she's been married so many times. Her uncle calls her Marlie."

"Has she lived there very long?" Jeanie asked.

"She's never lived any place very long. I'm no friend

of hers," she defended herself. "I've no use for her—no use at all. That's her uncle's place, and old John Matson is a hard-working man—never misses a day on his job at the stockyards. But she's—oh, she's here, there, everywhere, Arizona, California—until she gets down and out. And then back she comes to sponge off the poor old man."

"But she's got a job," Katie Rose said. "She sells dog food."

The woman's laugh was more of a grunt. "Not now, she doesn't. She takes a job that sounds like easy money, and then when she has to work at it—thuh!—she can't be bothered."

None of this sounded hopeful to Katie Rose for her collecting the fourteen dollars and fifty cents. She asked, "Do you know what time she'll be home? Or where we could find her?"

Again that belittling laugh. "Oh, everybody around here knows where she can be found this time of day. At the Little Shoe Tavern. Most likely she'll be there with that man she's running after. She meets him when he gets off work at the garage and filling station next door."

No doubt the woman would have leaned on her lawn mower and imparted more about her flighty neighbor. But Jeanie had evidently heard enough. "Come on, Katie Rose," she said.

They thanked the woman, and went back through the wagon-wheel gate and to the little car pulled half-way off the road. "Well, chum, that's that," Jeanie said as she climbed into the car.

Katie Rose's chin squared stubbornly. "I need the money she owes. And I don't want to have this long trip out here for nothing—absolutely nothing. Supposing we tracked her down to that Little Shoe bar—remember we passed it? Maybe—well, maybe if she wouldn't pay all the fourteen fifty, she might pay some—especially if she's with a man she's trying to make a hit with. Even ten bucks would be a lifesaver."

A moment's hesitation, and then Jeanie said on an edgy laugh, "I'm game to try it."

"We'll go quick before we lose our nerve," Katie Rose said, and started down Pinhorn Road.

They stopped in front of the cluster of buildings at the crossroads. Creamery, shoe repair shop, garage with filling station in front and, next to it, the Little Shoe Tavern. They looked at the cars already parked in front. Yes, there was the weathered and dusty brown and pink one with its rumpled fenders. "Arizona license," Jeanie muttered.

Katie Rose took from her billfold the pale blue bill from the Washington camera shop. The two hesitated a shaky moment outside the door on which was printed, YOUR FRIENDLY TAVERN. It was

Jeanie who said, "Come on. She can't do more than bang a bottle at us," and opened the door.

The tavern was small and dimly lighted. Behind the bar proper, the bartender was talking to a man relaxed on a high stool. They both turned curious eyes on the two girls who entered, and the bartender asked, "Can I do something for you?"

"We're looking for someone," Katie Rose said hastily.

Only a few people were at the small tables at the side. The blond woman they sought was not among them. At the end of the bar two booths had been crowded in. On one of them a man's cap, the kind worn by filling station attendants, hung on the hook.

Katie Rose and Jeanie walked toward it until they were in full view of its occupants. The man and woman, both on the same side of the table, were crowded as close together as it was possible for two people to be. The man was on the outside, and Katie Rose noted the name WALT lettered in red on his gray workshirt.

But it was the woman her eyes rested on, doubting briefly that she was the one they were looking for. She was not wearing the dress with its gaudy flowers, but an orange sunback with black shoulder straps no wider than shoe laces. But there was no mistaking that disheveled and chalky blond hair.

Her head was bent while she stabbed out a cigarette. She seemed to be having trouble connecting the cigarette with the spilling-over ashtray. The man saw them first. He grinned, and said thickly, "Hello, you little cuties. If you're looking for me, I'm off duty."

Katie Rose said, "We came to see *her*."

"Well, sit down—sit down," he urged expansively, his words slurring together. "Any friends of Marlie's are friends of mine. You sit right down and have a beer."

They didn't accept the invitation. The woman looked up. It took a minute for her eyes to focus on first Katie Rose and then Jeanie, and for recognition to dawn in them. Katie Rose was thinking, She can't bolt and run without pushing that big, grinning ape out first—

She was not bolting this time. Fortified perhaps by drink and her male companion, she drew herself up and said haughtily, "These are not my friends—they are not my friends at all. I don't want anything to do with them." The Grand Duchess manner sat ill on someone with narrow shoulder straps lopping down both arms and an untidy tuft of hair over one eye. She indicated Jeanie, "She's only trying to make trouble for me. Get her out of here, Walt."

"Don't you worry, sweetie," he mumbled. "S'all right. Nobody's going to make trouble."

"She thinks—she thinks—I'm afraid of her. Okay, so I made a mistake—but what can anybody do now— not after all these years—" Again she turned her eyes to Jeanie, and drew her drunken dignity about her, "I know all about the law on that. It's all past—"

Jeanie was staring at her in spellbound horror.

Walt muttered helpfully, "Everybody makes mistakes. What's past is past. Let the dead past bury its dead— I always say."

The woman's voice was shriller now as she turned to Jeanie, "Yeh, your father thinks he's God—just because he's a doctor. What'd he expect me to do—watch you every minute? Yeh, he thought I ought to sit by your bed and watch you breathe? Well, I had other things to—to—think about—and do—" She was screaming now.

The bartender appeared at the table, "What's the trouble here?" he asked.

"No trouble, Charlie," Walt assured him. "Jus' old friends getting together. Bring our little friends a beer—" and he motioned widely toward the two girls.

"I'd have to see their I.D. cards before I serve them."

The woman screamed out, "You don't need to see any I.D. cards. I know how old *she* is," and she pointed at the silent Jeanie. "She was sixteen the first of April—April Fool's Day—" and she laughed raucously.

A small gasp came from Jeanie as though a fist had landed in her middle. Katie Rose felt a tug at her arm. "Let's get out of here," Jeanie said.

They walked out the door, the shrill maudlin voice still in their ears. Jeanie's face had a gray pallor as though she were about to be sick to her stomach. They got in the car without noticing that the sky had turned lowering and black. Katie Rose was still clutching the pale blue bill from Miguel's camera shop in Washington. She had never once thought of it from the time they entered the tavern and stopped at that corner booth.

"What are you hanging on to that for?" Jeanie said on a harsh laugh. "You might as well tear it up and throw it into Little Shoe Creek—if we only knew where Little Shoe Creek keeps itself." And she laughed on in wild hysteria.

Katie Rose looked at her in amazement— But wasn't it Blake who'd written, "Excess of sorrow laughs"?

Jeanie was still laughing when lightning ripped across the sky and was followed by a heavy rumble of thunder. The very emergency of the threatened storm took their minds off the ugly and bewildering scene they had just left.

"Should we put the top up, Jeanie, or try to race the storm home?"

"Let's go. What do we care if we get soaked?"

"You'll have to watch the turns for me."

"I'll watch them." Jeanie added in a heavy voice, "I don't want to go home. I'll go home with you."

"If Liz is back from the doctor's, she'll have a pot of tea ready."

Jeanie sat silent as the car sped southward, with lightning and thunder overhead. She said only a time or two, "Turn right at the next corner," or "No—go on, and you'll catch a through street."

The lightning was more vicious and the snackle of thunder closer when Katie Rose and Jeanie hurried from the car and through the Belford picket gate.

The house was quiet. The kitchen seemed dark, what with the black sky overhead and the bamboo curtain pulled between kitchen and dinette. Katie Rose reached for the teakettle, and to make conversation, said, "Whew, that's a long old drive out there. Look at the time. I thought Liz would be home—and Ben must be working late."

Jeanie didn't answer that. She stood at the sink, silent as a statue, so that Katie Rose had to reach around her to fill the teakettle. She couldn't bear to see the stony suffering in her face, and she said, "Did you ever hear such senseless jabber as that woman was talking? Of course she was looped."

Jeanie didn't answer that either, but flung out chal-

lengingly, "Now do you still believe all that claptrap
Mom told about my being left on the chair at Mount
Carmel with a sweet little note tucked under the blanket. Now do you believe me when I said my father
knew who she was, and that she was no good—and
that's why—"

"Jeanie! You surely can't think that awful mess of
a woman is—is—?"

"My mother? What would you think, goose girl?
You heard her say when I was born." Her voice was
high-pitched and raw with feeling. "What do you
think she was talking about when she said she'd made
a mistake? You heard her say my father thought
that he was God—and expected her to sit beside
me and watch me breathe. And that grinning hyena
with her putting in about the dead past burying its—
its dead—"

She stopped suddenly, and her features twisted.
"Listen to me screeching like this. I must have inherited it from—from—" and suddenly great sobs
choked her.

She leaned against the sink, her small body con-
vulsed with them. Katie Rose put her arms around her.
She was at such a loss for words that she could only
say, "No, Jeanie, no—I don't believe it. It can't be
true—"

Jeanie's strangled voice was saying, "I'd be so ashamed for anyone to know. Promise me, Katie Rose, that you won't tell anyone—not Ben, not Liz—I couldn't even tell Mom or Dad—"

"Jeanie, don't—don't believe it. There must be some other reason why—" But there were so many unanswered *whys,* she thought.

The downpour of rain came with a roar like pounding hoofs on the roof. Katie Rose exclaimed, "Oh, my towels—I left them on the line. They'll get soaked!"

"Bring them in," Jeanie gulped out. "I'll go wash my face."

Katie Rose ran through the hard peppering of raindrops to the clothesline. She snatched the yellow guest towels off first. She bundled them all into her arms, and raced into the back door which opened into the dinette.

As she dropped her load on the table, she gave a gasp of amazement. Liz was asleep on the wide cushioned bench that ran along the wall.

She sat up blinking. "Oh, love, I should have thought of your washing. But I came back from the doctor's so bone-weary I just dropped down here for a minute."

Katie Rose looked at her closely. "Did you hear

Jeanie and me come in?" She meant, Did you hear Jeanie's outburst?

Liz said around a yawn, "You know, childeen, I think there's something in that shot the doctor gives me for my blood pressure—I swear it's like knockout drops. Hang your towels in the bathroom and they'll be dry in no time. I'll be making the tea."

FIFTEEN

The littles and Stacy came in drenched, and had to scamper up the stairs and into dry clothes. Ben was late. His "pour of cement" had been delayed by the downpour.

Everyone made for the dinette and Liz's hot tea in the big earthenware teapot. Again Katie Rose realized that no one could serve tea in the living room with fancy accompaniments unless that someone had nothing else to do.

Dear knows, she had tried off and on all these weeks, but they hadn't come off. It took such a multitude of dainty sandwiches and those assorted (and expen-

sive) cookies to stay her hungry crew till dinner time.
It took extra hours of making ready and then cleaning
up afterwards. Her elegant teas had gone the way of
her fruit centerpiece. Why did life have to be full of
compromises?

Surely in all the crowded confusion at the dinette
table, no one but Katie Rose noticed Jeanie's red eyes.
Surely no one but she noticed that Jeanie sat hugged
into her own unhappiness, and left the talking to everyone else.

The littles were telling about their lawn-cutting job
this afternoon, and the woman who claimed they had
nicked a blade of her lawn mower.

"Did you?" Ben demanded.

Both boys squirmed. Jill said, "Well, her old lawn
was full of dog bones and if it got nicked, it wasn't
our fault."

"You could have picked up the bones," Ben said.
"Did she pay you for cutting her lawn?"

The three nodded. "It was after she paid us that
she came running after us to tell us about her nicked
blade."

"Have you still got the money?"

They had part of it. They'd spent some at Downey's
Drug for chocolate sodas.

"All right," Ben said firmly. "The first thing in
the morning, you go over and tell her you'll take her

mower up to the bicycle shop on the Boulevard and have it fixed. It might be a sharpening will smooth out the nick—"

Jeanie interrupted on a derisive laugh, "Ben, you're my father over again. Pontifical. Go ahead and stress what makes good citizens."

Ben turned puzzled eyes on her. He said shortly, "I hate people that eel out of—well, things like that."

"The words are 'accepting responsibility,'" Jeanie mocked. "Oh, there are a lot more—'integrity,' 'duty,' 'self-sacrifice.' I've been brought up on them all." She stood up suddenly. "I'm going home," she said, and started for the door.

Ben put down his cup with a clatter. "I'll take you in the car. It's still raining."

"I don't want you to take me. I can walk—I don't care if it's raining."

The lines of Ben's jaw tightened. He was not called old bossy Ben for nothing. "I'm taking you whether you want it or not," and he fastened a firm hand on her arm.

Katie Rose sat on at the dinette table, her heart echoing Jeanie's jolt and heartache. She was still there when Ben returned. He looked hurt and troubled. "What's got into Jeanie to make her so snappish and on the prod?"

But Jeanie didn't want Ben to know what was gnawing at her vitals. Katie Rose only said, "Oh—she doesn't like her job very well. She says sending bills out gets pretty monotonous."

Katie Rose sat on while Liz puttered about. Stacy came down and wanted to discuss *A Doll's House.* "I read the whole thing through, and there isn't even a doll's house in it."

Alone at the table, Katie Rose slumped down on the dinette bench. She was weighted with Jeanie's worry, and wearied by the long tense drive. As her heavy eyes closed she was thinking: I'll just rest a minute. I'll have to wait till Perry pays me—and then get something—for dinner—something ready to serve— because I—won't have time—to—cook—

She was wakened by a sudden commotion of voices, the rattle of paper, and clink of metal beyond the bamboo screen.

Katie Rose's enemy boarder had come home.

By the time she reached the kitchen he was surrounded by the littles, Stacy, and Liz. He was taking from their cartons two pressure cookers, and reading directions from their accompanying booklets. "We'll put the beans to soak for the fifteen minutes we give the meat a head start," he announced.

Liz promptly rattled out a bowl for him.

He said blithely to Katie Rose, "You don't mind if I conduct an experiment here, do you? I have to report on the comparative merits of these two cookers. So I bought two pork hocks, and we'll cook two cups of beans in each one."

She tried to read his motive behind those opaque, hazel eyes. Was he doing this to give her budget a boost, knowing how low her funds were? Or to show her how cheaply he, old know-it-all, could feed eight people?

But what could she say when everyone was so carried away by his enthusiasm? One of the littles said, "Goody. We haven't had beans for a long, long time." If she said, "Try your experiments someplace else," she'd have to add, "But give me your board money, so I can buy groceries for dinner."

She said nothing.

The two cookers and their contents bubbled and hissed and gave out a delectable odor for some forty minutes.

A fine loyal family she had! "Nothing like a boiled dinner on a drizzly evening," Liz said. They all fell to with gusto when Perry McHarg's dinner was put on the table. All but Katie Rose. She wouldn't give him the satisfaction of either consuming or praising. She was hungry, and her mouth fairly watered when she was passed the bowl of mealy lima beans, but she said frigidly, "No thanks. I never liked boiled beans." He had made cabbage slaw too.

It was when she and Liz were washing the dishes that Liz asked, "Did you find that flighty vixen when you drove out to Pinhorn Road?"

"She wasn't home."

"She wasn't now? I was in hopes you'd find out what possessed her to bang the boyeen's camera. And didn't you see her at all?"

"We saw her. Because a woman across the road said she'd be at the Little Shoe Tavern. She was there all right, but we didn't get any money out of her."

"The Little Shoe Tavern," Liz repeated.

Again Katie Rose looked closely at Liz's bland face. But Liz was washing one of the pressure cookers which the Hotel and Restaurant Management school had entrusted to one of its students for testing. Liz said, "He marked this with a strip of adhesive because it cooked the beans in two minutes less time than the other."

"Phooey!" said Katie Rose.

When she went into the dining end of the big front room, Perry was sitting there with that hateful notebook open in front of him. She picked up the lacy table mats, shook them fiercely, and put them in the sideboard. She couldn't resist saying, "Don't forget to add the head of cabbage."

"I didn't. Seventeen cents. One of our teachers used to be a buyer for a chain of hotels, and he told me of a market down near the truck docks where you can buy things cheap. This supper tonight only cost two and a half dollars, and it fed eight people."

"Seven. I didn't eat any." (She'd wait until he went to his room and typewriter to satisfy her hunger.)

"But there was some left," he reminded her. "It would have fed eight generously, which figures about thirty-one cents per person."

Maddening, that's what he was. So when he handed her his board money, she sneered, "You forgot to take out for your greasy beans."

"That's all right," he said cheerfully. "I'll charge that off to research for my paper on marketing."

His outsmarting her still rankled the next morning when she buttered his toast. Today was Ben's eighteenth birthday. In all the jumble of happenings, Katie Rose had forgotten it. Ben said wryly, "Maybe we'd better keep it quiet. Grandda gave my boss to think I was already eighteen when he hired me."

But there was no keeping a birthday quiet in the Belford household. Stacy said, "Let's have a whingding birthday supper. We don't have to ask what your favorite food is, Ben."

Mother always had the birthday child's favorite menu for the birthday dinner. For the littles, it was spaghetti; for Stacy, chicken. Although steak was a rare item, Mother somehow managed Ben's favorite on his birthday.

Ben said now, "This friend of mine, Hank, who works with me—we decided to wait till noon to see if we were called on the job. If we're not, we'll play tennis and if it's all right, Katie Rose, I'd like to bring him home to dinner."

"Sure, bring him."

Wonderful, wonderful, she thought. Ben had told her about Hank. He was a college student and a lit major. She could hold a literary conversation with him and ignore her price-minded boarder.

Stacy said eagerly, "Can I ask Bruce too, Katie Rose? I've been wanting to ever since the Seeries had me out to his party."

Katie Rose nodded. She got up and reached for Mrs. McHarg's menus. Thumbing through them, she came to her birthday dinner for Mr. McHarg. "We'll have tenderloin tips and—"

"Not tenderloin tips, girl!" exclaimed Perry Mc-Harg. "That's the most expensive steak you can buy. Good Lord, for ten people!"

"And Jeanie," Liz said. "You'll be asking her, Ben?"

He bent his head over his plate. "I did ask her. The answer was no."

Katie Rose said, "Oh, but yesterday she was—well, sort of down in the dumps, Ben. I'll stop and see her when I go marketing and I'll talk her into coming."

Another time Ben would have said, "I'll do my own asking." This morning he gave her only a helpless and hopeful flick of his eyes.

"Tenderloin tips," she repeated. "And french fries, corn on the cob—"

"Not corn on the cob," said her nemesis. "It's still shipped in from Texas. Wait till we have homegrown."

"—and Caesar salad," went on Katie Rose as though there had been no interruption.

"What's Caesar salad?" Liz asked.

"It's the emperor of green salads," Perry answered. "To make a production out of it, you bring the bowl of greens to the table, and toss in all the thises and thatses—such as crumbled bacon and croutons, and you break in an egg that's been coddled for one minute only."

"Will you do the tossing, Perry, so my Big Romance will be impressed?" Stacy asked.

"Sure. I'll bring home a chef's cap for the job." But he turned to Katie Rose again. "There are other cuts of steak. How about my taking you to that market I was telling you about?"

That was all she needed to bolster up her own wavering doubt about those tenderloin tips. "*I'll* do the marketing," she said.

Perry left for school. So did Stacy. The littles went

reluctantly to make things right with the woman who blamed them for nicking one of her mower blades. Ben said, "Katie Rose, I'll pay you my ten now instead of waiting till Saturday. It looks like I might not get regular work for a few days."

Liz reached into the pocket of her skirt and drew out a twenty-dollar bill. "When you're shopping, child, would you mind stopping at the May Company and matching some yarn for me? My, how that afghan does eat it up."

"You can come with me, Liz."

"No, pet, I'll give you a sample of the yarn and the number. This new partial the dentist put in is bothering me. I may have to go down and have him work on it."

Katie Rose drove off in the Triumph deep in thought. There would be ten at the table this evening —eleven, if Jeanie came. She had only eight of the amber glasses, plates, and lacy mats. It would never do to ask the littles to eat at the dinette table—not on Ben's birthday. This was an extra special occasion with Ben bringing home Hank, the lit major. And Stacy asking Bruce Seerie. You could bet the Seeries never filled in with mismatched glasses and old round china plates.

She was still saying to herself, "No, I'd better not," and "But the table will look terrible if I don't," when in the needlework department at the May Company she took out Liz's yarn for matching. A clerk told her they were temporarily out of that number. "We're expecting a new shipment in any day."

Almost without volition, Katie Rose's feet turned to China and Glassware on the same floor. They still had amber glasses and plates. And the place mats. Now that the eighty-eight-cent sale was over, they could be bought only in cartons of four. For three forty-nine.

Again Katie Rose's dream took over. . . . Travel-weary Mother and Gran coming home. In the dream, Katie Rose said, "Now you two go up and rest, and I'll call you when dinner is ready." In the dream, she saw the awed unbelief on their faces when they came down and saw the table with its flower centerpiece, and candles gleaming on golden glassware. And in that instant, Mother would pay tribute to Katie Rose's way of running a house. . . .

She bought additional glasses, plates, and table mats. She took them with her.

She didn't have to drive to Harmony Heights to see Jeanie.

On the first floor of the store a booth was set up where people could buy or collect their season tickets for the Acacia Gardens Theater. Jeanie was just turning away from it with a slim envelope of tickets.

Katie Rose deposited her tied-together cartons at her feet. "I'm gathering together everything for Ben's birthday dinner. Please come, Jeanie."

Jeanie shook her head slowly. Her eyes were heavy in her thin oval face. Even the thick cinnamon-brown hair seemed a heavy weight on her head.

"What'd you and Ben fight about, for heaven's sake?"

Jeanie carefully put the tickets in her purse, and said in lackluster voice, "I wish I knew. Oh, Katie Rose, I never thought I'd be the kind to hurt other people just because I hurt so inside. I'm even afraid to be around him—I'm afraid I'll break down and tell him—"

"You can't pull into a shell just because—because— Come on over for Ben's birthday. He'd be tickled to death."

"We've got tickets for the show tonight. Cornelia Otis Skinner is out there. And Dad got the bright idea of our going out and having dinner first." She flicked a dismal smile, "Sort of a cure-all for my being so mopey last evening. Everything is so different. I mean Mom and Dad don't seem the same to me. I don't even seem the same myself."

"Did you say anything about—"

"That messy female? I did not! And I never intend to." Her lips curled. "I hope she elopes with that smirking Walt and goes to Africa or Afghanistan."

Katie Rose could think of nothing to say except, "Do you have time to grocery shop with me?"

Again Jeanie's lackluster voice, "No. That heavy rain all but pounded Mom's gladioluses into the ground. I have to hunt up stakes and see if I can tie them back in place." She turned and left without her usual, "Be seeing you," or "I'll phone you."

SIXTEEN

In the supermarket Katie Rose made her purchases.
Romaine and leaf lettuce for the Caesar salad. Frozen
french fries; she knew from experience that though
each package said it would serve four, she could count
on it to serve two with Belford appetites. She sacked
ten ears of the corn Perry McHarg said was shipped
in from Texas. There were always eggs, butter, bread,
cheese, and bacon to buy.

At the meat counter she saw only two packages of
tenderloin tips. She rang the bell for the butcher, and
when he shoved aside the glass window, asked him if
he had more. Yes, he would be glad to cut them for

her. How many did she need? Ten, she told him. Yes, ten.

She watched him toss the sizeable pile of them onto the scales and wrap them. She watched his black grease pencil write on the wrapping, $12.27.

Over twelve dollars— Wow! No wonder that even for the McHargs, tenderloin tips were a special-occasion item. Well, she would bake Ben's birthday cake instead of buying it at a bakery. She picked out package cake mix, and minute icing.

She checked out at the cashier's, and was heartened to see all the bills she had left in her billfold. Why, she had nothing to worry about—nothing at all. Especially when on Saturday everyone was going to Bannon for Cherry Day which would be a day of—to put it bluntly—freeloading. Even Perry McHarg planned on going.

A pleasant surprise awaited her at home. Ben's friend Hank was there though Ben was not. She had pictured a lit major as studious and spectacled, but the boy who leaped out of the porch chair and relieved her of her sacks of groceries was ruddy and blond with a carefree and winning grin.

He explained as they put the perishables in the refrigerator that Ben had received a call from the construction company. "He'll be hauling gravel today to replace the roadbed the cloudburst washed out yesterday. But I stuck around waiting for Ben's beautiful sister to play tennis with me."

The admiration in his eyes was healing balm to her ego that Perry McHarg had rubbed raw. "Oh! Couldn't they use you for hauling gravel?"

"I didn't bother to find out. I decided I'd had enough hard labor for one summer. Some fellows I know are taking off for California tomorrow morning, and I didn't want to miss out on the fun. I'm not the glutton for work old Ben is."

Katie Rose felt a passing pang for Ben. There was no deciding for him that he'd had enough hard labor for one summer—not when he was hoarding his money for entering the university in September.

"Better throw in a swimsuit along with your tennis racket," Hank told her.

She changed into her best red-striped T-shirt and white shorts. She took Ben's tennis racket. Grateful that Stacy was at the school library and not at Coral Sands, she took her white satin suit and petaled cap.

"I'm not much of a tennis player," she said as she settled beside him in the front seat of his car.

"You can't be everything," he said meaningfully.

They didn't play much tennis after all. A sudden shower drove them into the park pavilion where they dawdled over hot dogs and Cokes. The sun came out once more, and they decided on swimming.

She need make no apologies about her swimming.

In the four hours they spent together, he paid her more compliments than Perry McHarg had in the over four weeks he had been under their roof. Hank had whistled and pretended to swoon when she emerged from the locker rooms in the white swimsuit. When they rested on the beach, *he* noticed that her eyes had a violet cast and quoted,

> *They smile, and lost in dreaming*
> *I cannot say a word.*

"That's Heine," she said, and he let out a glad whoop. "You know Heine? Katie Rose, I never dared hope you'd be both pretty and poetic."

And he wasn't so "lost in dreaming" that he could "not say a word." Katie Rose's sensible side took all his praiseful build-up for what it was; her Irish kin had a word for it, "palaver." But she liked it just the same.

These had been trying days. That cold war between her and her severest critic. And poor Jeanie so un-Jeanielike that Katie Rose didn't even have the relief of spilling out her own vexations to her.

So she sat on the sand, delighting in his flattery. She noticed how the shadows were lengthening, and she stood up and said, "The steaks, the steaks are calling—"

" 'From glen to glen and down the mountainside,' "
he sang back.

"Oh my goodness—the birthday cake! I was going
to bake one for Ben."

"That's what bakeries are in business for," he said.

She stopped and bought one with a fluffy white
icing on their way home.

Perry McHarg was already in the kitchen when she
carried it in. "I came home early to help with Ben's
birthday dinner," he told her. "I'll be Pierre, the
maître d'." Not only was a white chef's cap tilted on
top his head, but he wore a white apron.

Hank said he would only be an impediment in the
kitchen, and turned his attention to the record player
in the front room.

Katie Rose was grateful for Perry's expert help in
assembling all the makings for the Caesar salad and
carrying them to the card table he set up close to the
dining one.

She took time out from the meal preparations to
sternly admonish the littles, "Wash up and dress up,
the three of you. We're having company for Ben's
birthday. And, Jill, don't you dare come down in
Levi's."

Ben came home from his truck driving. Katie Rose
saw his eyes swiftly count the places that were set.
She stretched the truth a little, and said, "Jeanie would

have loved to come. But you know how her folks always go to the show at Acacia Gardens on Wednesday."

Liz returned from her session with the dentist. She leaned in the kitchen doorway, and smiled wearily at the two workers. "I see you've got help, lovely. I might stretch out a few minutes."

Perry said, "Do that, Liz—you look pretty beat. We'll call you when soup's on."

At times like this when Perry seemed so one of them, it was easy for Katie Rose to forget they were enemies. She forgot it again when he nudged her and said low, "I wish you'd look."

He meant Jill. She had descended the stairs not only in her wrap-around denim and white blouse, but she had stopped in front of the hall mirror to struggle with tying the green tie that went with the blouse. Perry said, "Here, Jill, let me. I'm an old bow-tyer from 'way back."

In the kitchen again, he said, "We'll season the steaks before we put them under the broiler." Katie Rose quickly unwrapped them to keep him from seeing the price. But he took the paper from her, smoothed it out and read those black figures.

"Just like chewing up dollar bills," he muttered darkly. "Sometimes I think you haven't the sense God gave a little green apple."

The cold war was on again.

But the dinner party couldn't have been more successful. Everyone was impressed, even Bruce Seerie, Stacy's bronze athlete, at the expert and loving way Perry seasoned and tossed the salad. And at Katie Rose's amber plates holding the juicy steaks, french fries, and ears of corn. (Liz's new dental work kept her from eating either her steak or corn.)

Another thing gladdened Katie Rose's heart and added to her triumph. That was Hank's continued admiration, his well-turned compliments. She hoped Perry McHarg took note.

Stacy was airing her puzzlement over *A Doll's House*. "I still have to write a three-page report on it. But what'll I say? I read every word of it, and I couldn't find a doll's house anyplace. That's what mizzled me."

"She always pronounces 'misled' like that," Katie Rose told the amazed Hank. "She says the word looks as though it *ought* to be mizzled. She's terrible. And the awful part of it is, we copy her without realizing it. She calls Pikes Peak 'Piker's Peak,' and one day I called it that in school—"

Stacy broke in, "Hank, you're a lit major, so you tell me what the play is about. Our teacher said it had great significance."

He side-stepped that by saying, "Ask Katie Rose.

She knows more about plays and poetry than I do. Tell her, beautiful."

Ah, here was her chance. She elucidated, "The significance of it is that in those days women were expected to be dumb. They were supposed to let *men* give them orders. And Nora revolted because she was sick of being treated as though she were a little nitwit —or Miss Idiot of the Year—and I don't blame her—"

Perry McHarg nudged her. "Go light the candles on the cake while I clear off the plates."

A surprising thing happened when Katie Rose was bringing in the cake with the eighteen candles lighted. Jeanie Kincaid came in the front door bearing a sheaf of gladioluses.

Unpredictable Jeanie! She said, "I can't stay but a minute—we're late now because Dad had to make a call—but I wanted to say 'Happy Birthday, Ben—'"

He was up from the table and by her side, and she thrust the flowers into his hands and said with a catch in her voice, "It's a fool present to give anybody—I even had to strip off the bruised ones—but I just wanted to—to—"

Ben stared at her wonderingly. "I don't even know what kind of flowers they are—but it's a swell present, Jeanie." And for a brief moment they looked at each other over the flowers, and it was as though he said, "Your coming was the best present I could have," and that she said, "Bear with me, please, Ben—I don't mean to be hateful to you."

And then she hurried out to join her parents in the waiting car.

The "Happy Birthday, Dear Ben" was sung and the cake cut. The table was cleared and the dishes washed. Perry McHarg went to the typewriter in his room. Bruce Seerie asked Ben if he and Stacy could drive down to the park to listen to the band concert and watch the colored fountain.

Hank asked Katie Rose to go with him to the Red Barn. "I couldn't leave for California without dancing with you," he said. "So put on your fluffy ruffles and enchanting smile."

She put on her fashion-show dress.

The Red Barn, lighted by lanterns hung from rafters, with rough plank tables lining the wall, and its hillbilly band, was the gathering place for the high-school and college crowd. Hank ran into many of his friends and their dates. Tables were pushed together to accommodate them all.

And while she danced with Hank, she ran into someone who was not exactly a friend, but who greeted her loudly with, "Katie Rose! Where've you been keeping yourself? I never see you at Wetzel's anymore."

It was Rita Flood. The boy she was dancing with

was one of those who prided himself on staying away from a barbershop, and on being sullen—and not too well washed. He merely glowered at Katie Rose while Rita went on, "I'm getting paid tomorrow night—" again her covetous eyes traveled over Katie Rose's dress of cotton lace, "And I'll be down for the pattern so's I—"

Hank whirled her past.

Such a gay evening. Hank's flattery never ran down. He pretended to be jealous when his friends danced with Katie Rose. He told her that if she'd say the word he wouldn't leave for California at five in the morning. Strange, that Katie Rose should feel the purple pumps pinching her feet. And that every now and then Jeanie's tormented face rose up to haunt her.

It was one of Hank's traveling companions who said when the band took a break at eleven, "Let's get Lochinvar on his way, Katie Rose. All right if I ride home with you? We're leaving at dawn, and he hasn't even packed a toothbrush yet."

Hank escorted her to the Belford front door still protesting undying affection. She didn't believe a word of it, but it still made a delightful ending to the day.

SEVENTEEN

Katie Rose's staggering blow came the next morning.

They were at breakfast when Liz asked, "Did you get my yarn, lovey, at the May Company yesterday?"

Katie Rose looked at her blankly. The yarn? Liz's yarn for her afghan had never once entered her mind again from the minute she left the needlework department of the store until now.

"They didn't have it, Liz. But they're expecting it in any day."

Liz went on with a sigh, "I'd hoped I wouldn't have to refill that blood-pressure prescription at Downey's Drug. The price of it!—you'd think they made it out of gold tailings." She turned to the littles, "Now if Katie Rose gives you my twenty, will you be careful of the change?"

Again Katie Rose's mind went blank. Liz's twenty? Liz's handing her the twenty-dollar bill had completely slipped her mind until this very minute. Liz added, "Come to think of it, I'll walk down myself and see if they've any new murder mysteries, and visit with Pearl at the bakery."

Katie Rose got up from the table and went into the kitchen. She took her billfold off the refrigerator where she had left it last evening. She opened it on what had seemed such a heartening array of bills after paying the cashier at the supermarket. And so it was, except that the ten, the five, and the five ones didn't belong to her. She must have crumpled up some bills and thrust them in the coin part. Hastily she unsnapped it. Only a dime, two nickels, and three pennies nestled there.

She handed Liz her money with a murmured, "I had to break your twenty-dollar bill," and dropped back into her place, dazed. It wasn't possible! She had started out with Perry's eighteen, and Ben's ten. She couldn't—she simply couldn't!—have spent all but twenty-eight cents for a birthday dinner.

Well—yes—she could have, when you thought of the amber plates, glasses, and the woven place mats.

And the tenderloin tips—*and* the birthday cake which she hadn't taken time to bake.

She glanced at Perry McHarg who was taking his last forkful of egg. She shoved the billfold deeper into her lap, fearful that his X-ray eyes might see the pittance left in it.

Ben was turning the pages of the morning *Call*. She heard him say without really hearing him, "They didn't get it after all."

"Who didn't get what?" Stacy asked.

"The contract for a five-mile strip of Valley Highway. My boss told me he put in a bid on it. But it says here another road contractor got it."

"Will it mean less work for you?" Perry McHarg asked.

"It could. Oh well, the pay's good. I guess I won't hurt too bad if I lose a day now and then."

Katie Rose only sat, jolted and stunned and desperate. She sat on after the littles took off on a lawn-cutting job, and Ben for what might be a day's work or might not. And after Stacy left for school, and the hotel and restaurant management student departed in his station wagon with books, brochures, and those hateful notebooks.

Yes, it was that forgotten twenty of Liz's that had lulled her into a nice—but false—feeling of security. Twenty-eight cents. This was Thursday. And there would be no money forthcoming on Saturday because Ben had paid ahead, and Liz would be leaving before long. Dear Heaven, and *no* money from Perry Mc-Harg again. He was paid up until next Tuesday.

She got up on tottery legs and looked into the refrigerator. There were still eggs, bacon, and milk, and one package of frozen green beans. In the cupboard were two cans of mushrooms, one of chicken, and the cake mix and icing, still untouched from yesterday. On the sink drainboard sat a quarter of Ben's birthday cake. The littles would make short shrift of that this noon.

Feeble hope stirred in her. This was the Thursday of the Barton's supper and bridge. They'd surely need her to stay with Eva. She couldn't stand the suspense of waiting for Eva's daughter to phone, so she gathered her courage to call her and said with a brightness she didn't feel, "You'll be wanting me tonight, won't you, to stay with—"

"No, not tonight, Katie Rose. Our little get-together has been postponed until next week because two of the couples are on vacation."

Liz came down the stairs in her hat with buff roses and her best shoes for her visity trip to the Boulevard. Alone in the house, Katie Rose went from room to room, doing inept picky things.

Hindsight is much clearer than foresight. She

shouldn't have splurged so on those bath sets and the bath mat. And they could have done with fewer towel racks and toothbrush holders. She wished now that she had let Perry McHarg's bare feet touch the cold floor by his bed. Oh, to have that fifteen dollars of rug money back! She even thought longingly of those three dollars Pete Manzanares had so greedily snatched from her.

Wasn't there any straw for a drowning man to clutch?

Maybe—just maybe—the McHargs were back from the mountains and could use a baby-sitter. She dialed their number and let it ring—ring—ring. But there was no answer.

An unexpected straw came her way at noon, and she grabbed at it eagerly. Stacy came home from school and in between gulps of milk and bites of bread and jelly, told that her lit teacher had invited the class to her home this evening to watch a play on TV called *Hetty Garbler*—

"*Hedda Gabler*," Katie Rose corrected absently. "Ibsen's—the same one who wrote your *A Doll's House*."

"It'll be so helpful, said she, for us to make notes on the unfolding of character traits. Ha! The only helpful thing about it is that I've got an excuse not to baby-sit for Prince Charlie tonight. I'm going to call his fond mamma, and tell her it'll conflict with my literary education—"

"Wait, Stacy, wait! Don't phone. Let me go."

"*You* go?"

On previous occasions when Stacy had promised to sit elsewhere and Charlie's mother had phoned, Stacy had asked, "Katie Rose, do you want to take the prince tonight?" The prompt answer had always been, "No. He's all yours to take or leave."

For Stacy never came back from an evening there that she didn't explode about the prince's "allegories" and whims. "Oh, the *Hail Marys* I have to say to keep from telling off that fat little slob. Imagine a ten-year-old—that's practically as old as Brian—sitting in the tub and ordering me to scrub his back like an archbishop."

Mother had laughed at that. "I can't imagine an archbishop asking you to scrub his back."

But on this rock-bottom Thursday, Katie Rose repeated grimly, "I'll go."

"You'll have to prepare the prince's dinner because his folks are meeting friends on a five-thirty plane and they're all dining at the airport. What do you want to take it on for?"

"I need the money," she confessed. "But don't breathe it to Perry McHarg."

"You need money that bad?" And then in instant

generosity, "I've got a long night at the Novaks' Saturday night when they go to a school reunion dance. I told them Cherry Day at Bannon finished up at sundown, and I'd be back in time."

Cherry Day! Could a girl go to her hot-tempered grandfather and admit she was out on the limb he had predicted? It would be eating humble and very bitter pie after his flinging out, "And don't think you can come yelping for help from me," and her flinging back, "You needn't worry. You'd be the last one I'd go yelping to for help."

Stacy finished, "You can have all or any part of what the Novaks pay me Saturday. And you know what late stayer-outers they are."

But Saturday night seemed a long way off. Today and tomorrow were Katie Rose's immediate worry. "I'll fix dinner, and leave it for you to dish up," she told Stacy.

It took some scrimping and scrounging. She made French crepes, using three eggs instead of five, and adding more flour and milk to stretch the batter. For filling, she opened the small can of chicken, scraped every shred of meat off the pork hocks Perry McHarg had cooked night before last, and even added the piece of steak Liz had left untouched on her plate last evening. She cut the kernels off the ear of corn Liz had also left, and added it to the package of frozen green beans.

At least she wasn't there to see Perry's face when Stacy served it, for the prince's father picked her up at five.

The prince's mother was all uneasy flutter about a new baby-sitter being left with Charles. She had to show Katie Rose the greaseless skillet his chop must be cooked in, the certain soap for his bath. She took so long to tell her what she must do and must not do that she didn't tell her what time to expect them back.

Katie Rose wished she knew, so she could figure on how much she could add to her own measly twenty-eight cents. She left the kitchen to ask Charles, who had settled himself in front of the TV and his favorite show, "Did your folks say how long they'll be at the airport with their friends?"

"I'm not to be interrupted when I'm watching a show," he reprimanded her.

She cooked the lamb chops in the right skillet, salting and peppering them. Pepper didn't agree with him, he told her, and demanded that she scrape it off his chop. "I can still taste it," he said. "You'll have to cook me another one." She did, fuming inwardly.

They were finishing dinner when Brian came. He had ridden his bicycle over to tell her the glad news. At long last, the littles had found the woman at home who owed them for two months of the *Call*. They had divided the three dollars and a half between them.

"So, Katie Rose, I can pay you back a dollar of the three you had to pay that Pete—remember?"

A dollar was a dollar— it would seem even *two* to Katie Rose right now—but she shook her head. "No, Brian. Because it was my fault that we had to get the mice back."

What a noticeable contrast between the slim, tanned, hard-muscled Brian and the overweight, flabby, pampered Charles! Perhaps the protected one felt it too, for he said loftily, "Huh, do you think three dollars and a half is a lot of money? Wait till you see how much I've got."

He brought out his bank made of glass and with different slots for halves, quarters, dimes, and nickels. (It didn't bother with pennies.) It also had a device to register how much had been deposited. "See what it says? Seventeen dollars and forty cents, and I've only had it since my birthday in May. I was ten then."

Brian looked at all those beautiful half-dollars and quarters, and said nothing except, "Well, I guess I'd better be going." But at the door he paused to say, "Liz says she bets Mom and Gran will be home before we know it. Won't you be glad when Mom comes back?"

"Oh yes, Brian. I guess we've all been homesick for her."

Oh, but her dream—her beautiful dream of showing Mother her new and different way of cooking and serving meals. She felt a lump in her throat. It was so wrong, so ignoble for her regime to end not with a bang, but with a whimper.

The prince couldn't bear *not* to be noticed. He pushed up to Brian. "Is that awful old bike yours? I've got a brand-new one. I ride it up and down the sidewalk while Mother watches from the porch."

Brian gave him an unbelieving look. "Why does she watch you from the porch?"

"Because there are real mean boys in this block, and they ram their bicycles into me."

"You oughtn't to let them," Brian said almost gently. "When you see them making for you, you ram them first. Nobody rams us." He gave Katie Rose a look of both puzzlement and pity, swung onto his hard worn bicycle and rode off.

She could forgive her charge his snubbing remarks toward her, but not to Brian. So she ran his bath water in the tub and said briefly, "There you are," and started out the door.

"The baby-sitter is supposed to give me my bath."

"Baby-sitters are supposed to give babies baths, but not boys as old as you are."

Later when he emerged in pajamas and robe, he said sulkily, "I'd like to play checkers. I'm very good at games."

Katie Rose won the first game. He didn't like that. Maybe the baby-sitter was supposed to let him win. And she might have, just to keep peace, if he hadn't lorded it over Brian. Charles won the second. "This next one will decide the winner," he said, and sat back while she put the checkers on the squares.

The third game was long and drawn out. Charles's round face puckered in concentration over each move. But when it reached a point where Katie Rose had three kings and he had only two, she lured him out of the corner and jumped his two in one move.

He leaped up in rage, spilling all the black checkers in his lap onto the floor. Katie Rose fought against her impulse to bang him on the head with the board. Instead she folded it, and put her own checkers in the box.

"Pick up the black ones too," he screamed.

"I didn't throw them on the floor." She walked over and turned on the TV again.

He pouted in a corner of the couch for about five minutes before he picked them up and handed them to her. She was putting board and checkers in a cabinet when she noticed the pictures of two small children in two different frames on top of it.

"Whose pictures are these, Charles?" she asked.

"My brother and sister. They died before I was born. We don't have strong constitutions," he quoted.

It sobered Katie Rose. She remembered then that Charles's parents weren't as young as most of the parents she baby-sat for. She looked back at the framed pictures of children who were no longer alive. She could understand now why his mother and father treated their son as fragile and special cargo.

She said more kindly, "I noticed you had root beer and ice cream in the refrigerator. How'd you like me to mix you up a brown cow? I fix them for the littles at home."

"Does Brian like them?"

"Yes, he's crazy about them."

"I could try one. I guess it wouldn't hurt me."

His parents returned at eight. Oh dear, only three hours. Only a dollar and a half. She had hoped they would stay out until eleven or twelve.

EIGHTEEN

Who was it who had quoted, "Life is real, and life is earnest," to Katie Rose? Why, it was no less than Perry McHarg that first evening they had met at the McHargs' when she had made such a play for his attention. It seemed eons ago. Well, now she could add, "And life is terrifying."

Friday's breakfast cleaned out the icebox of milk, butter, and eggs. And bread out of the box.

Did Ben realize it was empty? Maybe. Because he said, "I won't take any lunch this morning. If I work longer than half a day, I'll pick up a bite someplace nearby."

What about the boarder? His course at the university finished today. She could scarcely keep from shouting at him as he went out the door, "Go back to Phoenix. Don't hang around here." But either way she was over a barrel. He had paid for a week, and if he left he might expect her to refund some of his board money. Which she didn't have.

Again she sat on at the dinette table. No use flicking through the McHarg file with its Friday menus of curried shrimp or lobster salad. Could she possibly manage her mother's *cheap and fillin'* macaroni and cheese?

She drew a sheet of paper toward her and wrote:

I've only got $1.78.

and under it,

3 pkgs. macaroni, 26¢ each	.78
1 lb. cheese	.79
4 loaves bread, 28¢ each	1.12
1 lb. butter	.79
1 gal. milk	.82

With a macaroni casserole, Mother always served canned tomatoes to double as both vegetable and salad. Katie Rose added sixty cents for two cans, and then totaled up her figures.

Four dollars and ninety cents! And that was only for dinner tonight. She still had eight hungry people to feed for breakfast in the morning before they left for Cherry Day at Bannon. She'd need bacon, eggs, cereal—

The blue slip from the camera shop in Washington was still folded in her billfold. She fingered it while her desperate thoughts raced in all directions. With sudden resolution she went to the telephone and dialed the Kincaid number, hoping to catch Jeanie before she left for her job. Jeanie answered.

She decided to lead up to what she had to say. "Jeanie, you didn't forget that tomorrow is Cherry Day at Bannon? Did you find an old-time dress you can wear? You're going with us, aren't you?"

"I sure am. I'd go anyplace to get as far out of town as I could—and for as long as I could. Dad is going to operate at eight in the morning, so he can drop me off at your house pretty early."

A pause, and then, "Jeanie, I'm suffering for money. I was thinking this—I just remembered Grandda telling about somebody that owed him money that he just couldn't make any headway in collecting—so he had a lawyer write and threaten to bring suit. He said—Grandda—that there was nothing like a letter with attorney-at-law at the top to put the fear of God in a deadbeat. And so I was thinking that I could ask

Beany's husband—you know, Carl?—to write a letter to the—the dog-burger woman about the money she owes for wrecking Miguel's camera—"

A gasp came from Jeanie's end, but Katie Rose went on, "I'd drive out there with it and just be real businesslike. I'll even tell her I'll settle for half—that'd be seven dollars and—"

Jeanie snapped, "Wait till I get on the phone in my room."

Katie Rose waited the brief while it took Jeanie to leave the living room, where no doubt her mother was within earshot, and walk down the hall to her own room. Jeanie's low vehement voice said, "Can't you let sleeping dogs—or sleeping dog-burger women— lie? I won't have her dragged out in the open. I won't have any adult noses stuck in—in that mess—"

"I've got to get some money. I'm just—"

"How mercenary can you get? To put my neck on the block for a few bucks you couldn't pry out of her anyway! If you mix Carl Buell up in this, or if you go out there hounding that—that female, I'll never speak to you again as long as I live! I mean it!" The phone banged down hard at her end.

Katie Rose was still standing there, feeling more helpless than before, when the phone rang. Jeanie said brokenly, "I'm sorry, Katie Rose—I'm sorry. I didn't mean to be so mean. Only please, I beg you—don't go near her—the very thought of her is more than—"

"All right, I won't."

To the old Jeanie she could have confessed, "I've got eight people to feed and I'm bankrupt." But this Jeanie who said a hasty good-by was too immersed in her own private grief.

She was slowly folding the blue paper and putting it back in her billfold when another forlorn hope was born. Those sacks of white and whole wheat flour, corn meal and oatmeal that she had so unceremoniously disposed of! She needn't make the lumpy Irish bread she had been so loud in denouncing, but she *could* stir up muffins or corn bread. She *could* serve oatmeal for breakfast tomorrow and say off-handedly, "I thought we needed a filling breakfast for our trip to Bannon."

She hurried to the basement and to the corner near the laundry tubs where she had deposited the heavy-duty paper sacks. They had all been about a fourth full.

She picked up the first one of whole wheat flour. The bottom dropped out of it, and so did its contents. For the love of heaven! She saw then the damp water stain on the other sacks.

For months there had been a small drip under the laundry tubs which hadn't seemed emergent enough for calling a plumber. Instead, Ben had taped the pipe with black adhesive. But there was still enough slow seepage to keep the cement floor in that corner constantly damp.

She scooped up a handful of oatmeal out of the sack. The flakes were swollen, and gave out a sour musty smell. So did the contents of the other sacks.

No hope for any face-saving here. And this, she thought sickly, was being hoisted on her own petard— her own petard being her joyful disposing of dollars' worth of flour and breakfast food.

She leaned against the cool soapstone of their old tubs engulfed by self-reproach. Her wanting to show off with slivered almonds, sour cream, spinach soufflé— oh, and those tenderloin tips!—had been her undoing.

Who could she turn to? Ben? She shook her head. It wasn't only his I-told-you-so she dreaded. But he had incurred aching muscles and blisters because it meant college tuition and books this fall. That morning he had paid his ten dollars in advance, he had gathered up the phone and the gas and light bills to pay. Ben had done more than enough.

Liz? No, not Liz. In her kindly way, she had tried to stem Katie Rose's reckless spending. She had looked at those packages of ready-baked waffles and murmured, "Six waffles it says on the box. Sure all of them put together would barely make a man-sized one." It was bad enough to have taken money from Liz when she was *family,* when she was forever making beds, washing dishes, and tidying up.

And now Katie Rose knew. It wasn't because her mother was fifty years behind the times that she didn't practice McHarg ways. She knew that to cook in quantity you had to buy in quantity. Maybe she too, tired from her night at the Gay Nineties, would have liked to buy apple torte from the dairy counter instead of garnering windfall apples from under their tree and making tarts from scratch. Mother had never felt she could afford the "built-in maid service" Perry McHarg was so glib about.

Perry. Ah, that was the bitterest pill! She wouldn't mind—well, not so much—facing the ignominy of failure with Ben and Liz—even Grandda—

Fifteen minutes and a lifetime later, Katie Rose slowly ascended the stairs. Liz said from the sink where she was rinsing out a cup, "Your grandda just stopped in. I gave him a cup of coffee. I wanted to call you, but he said he could only stay a minute— he had to pick up more lumber for the booths tomorrow. He'll be saving places for you girls in the stagecoach, he said. And he said he gave Aunt Kitty the fryers for the picnic supper—"

"Jeanie's going, too."

"Ah, that's nice. And nice that Perry is. There'll be food aplenty for all."

"Last Cherry Day I won a sack of groceries at the grocery booth," Katie Rose remembered aloud. "Nearly every year one of us wins one."

"And the tickets are only three for a quarter." Liz added, "Put coffee on your list, lovey. We're almost out."

Liz went out to visit over the fence with the next door neighbor. Katie Rose started up the stairs. Weighted with despair, she dropped down on the bottom step.

Someone stepped onto the porch and called through the front screen, "Katie Rose, are you home?" It was Rita Flood peering through the door. She saw the figure on the stairs and came in, announcing, "I want to get your pattern."

"The pattern? Oh, the pattern. But I don't know— I haven't had time to hunt for it yet."

"I told you a half-dozen times I wanted it. I'm going to get the stuff right away, and make it to wear tonight. Heavy date. Look, I just had my hair done. At Adrienne's on the Boul." She turned herself about, preening. "Well, lets find the pattern."

She followed Katie Rose up the stairs. In between the bottom step and the top one, desperation planted a thought in Katie Rose's mind. It persisted all the time Rita bragged about going to Acacia Gardens tonight—

"You'll never have time to buy the material and

have it made by this evening," Katie Rose said as they entered her room.

"I'm a fast worker—or didn't you know? How much did it cost you to make the dress?"

"The pattern and the lining and the cotton lace and zipper came to over seven dollars." Katie Rose took the dress from the closet. "The hem has to be whipped in by hand." And part of her mind was thinking: I can't—I just can't tell Rita I'll sell it to her. I can't bear to think of her flouncing around in my very best dress. But the other part of her mind was picturing the bare icebox and the dollar, seventy-eight in her purse.

Rita's greedy eyes were on the dress. Katie Rose swallowed hard, and she said lightly, "I don't know what the heck I did with that pattern. Mom might have lent it to somebody. But I was just thinking—if you want to buy the dress so you can wear it tonight, I'll sell it to you."

Rita said swiftly, "You will? How much?"

"For what it cost to make. Seven dollars."

She should have known it wouldn't be easy. She should have known Rita would sense she was out on a limb and make the most of it. "*Seven* dollars!" Rita discounted. "But it's second-hand. You ought to see the twenty-five and thirty dollar dresses you can buy at Goodwill for almost nothing."

"This isn't Goodwill," Katie Rose said shortly. It was only the lightness of her billfold in the pocket of her shorts that kept her from saying, "I wouldn't sell you my dress at any price."

"I'll give you six for the dress and belt and the shoes that match."

"The pumps? I didn't say I'd include the pumps for seven."

Rita laughed wisely. "Oh listen, you can't fool me. I'll bet your mother got them at a rummage sale for about two-bits."

The shame of having to haggle with her. "She paid fifty cents for them, and I paid a dollar seventy-five for the purple spray dye." Of course they did pinch her feet. She glanced at Rita's wide feet in tennis shoes, and said, "But I'll let you take them too," and she thought: I hope you get blisters from them.

"All right then," Rita agreed grudgingly. "Seven for the dress and shoes. How about the beads that go with it?"

"They're not mine—they're Mom's. Give me the seven dollars." And go, she longed to scream. For the sight of Rita holding the dress up to herself and pinching it in at her waist was almost too much for the seller.

Rita gave her the seven dollars, but she didn't go. She stood looking in the closet and this time her covetous eyes lighed on the short furry Prom Night jacket.

She reached in and took it out, and shuffed off the
pliofilm covering Katie Rose always tucked lovingly
about it. "Want to sell me this while you're at it? I
need something like it to wear—you know how chilly
it gets out at Acacia—?"

"No," Katie Rose said, and took it out of her hands.

"I'll give you another seven for it."

This time it was Katie Rose who screamed out,
"Seven! Are you crazy? Aunt Eustace gave it to me.
She bought it at Madeline's. It cost almost ten times
that much."

Rita shrugged. "It's worn. I've seen you wear it at
a lot of school shindigs. I'll give you seven fifty."

"I won't sell it." Katie Rose hung it back in the
closet and shut the door tight.

She left the room, and Rita had no choice but to
follow her. But when they walked down the stairs and
Katie Rose held the front door open for her—trying
not to look at the dress over her arm—Rita got in the
last word, "If you change your mind about that little
imitation fur deal of yours, let me know."

With shaky fingers Katie Rose put Rita's seven in
her billfold. She took her list and set out for Wetzel's
afoot. Even though Miguel's car was a small gas con-
sumer, she had no money to spare for even a gallon
this morning.

She glanced furtively at the cluttered Flood premises

as she approached the store. No Rita was in sight, thank heaven. Rita, the sharpie, might easily guess that she'd had to sell her dress and shoes for grocery money.

Both the store owners at Wetzel's gave her a chilly reception. It wasn't only because she had refused the backbones, but because they knew she had been making her purchases elsewhere.

Not a smile from Papa Wetzel as he carefully cut off a pound of cheese from a round that was nearing the end. Another time he would have said, "I'll just let you have the whole piece now it's getting hard to slice." Mamma Wetzel made no friendly inquiry as to how Ben was doing on his job or when Mother would be home, but reached for the items Katie Rose asked for and put them on the counter.

"Anything else?" she asked curtly.

Katie Rose was about to say, "Bread," when an inspired memory came to her. That sign in Pearl's Bakery announcing a cut price on day-old bread. She hoped this would be Pearl's morning off, so she wouldn't hear her ask for it.

"No, that's all, Mrs. Wetzel."

Mrs. Wetzel behind the cash register said, "Eight dollars and seventy-two cents."

Katie Rose stared joltedly at her, and then back to the sizeable array of groceries on the counter before her. She faltered, "But I don't—I don't have that much."

How many times in the past had Katie Rose bought more than she had money for! On those times one of the Wetzels always said easily, "That's all right. Pay it the next time you come in." But Mrs. Wetzel stood behind the counter, wordless and ungiving.

"I guess I'll get margarine instead of butter and—and just a half-gallon of milk instead of a gallon."

Mrs. Wetzel made the exchange, sacked the groceries, and gave Katie Rose twenty-four cents back from her eight dollars.

As she walked down the store steps she saw Rita in the Flood yard, sidestepping bent and rusty car parts to hang a pair of stockings on the clothesline. She hoped Rita wouldn't see her, but she hoped in vain. Rita called out jauntily, "How come you're not driving Miguel's little speedboat? How come you're buying stuff at Wetzel's? What I heard was that you were too hifalutin!"

What could Katie Rose answer to that? Nothing. So she busied herself adjusting the sack of groceries onto her hipbone and started the five-block walk to the Boulevard and bakery.

This wasn't her morning. Pearl was not only behind the counter but her first loud greeting in front of the storeful of customers was, "Katie Rose, don't you feed your littles enough at home? They're here every morning when the store opens to buy doughnuts."

Again Katie Rose swallowed a hard lump of humble pie, and asked for day-old bread. Pearl studied her a long minute. "I've got some *two*-day-old if you can use brown. It's the only kind I ever use for toast," she confided in her old friend-of-the-family way.

It was her forgiving kindness after the many buffetings of the morning that undid Katie Rose. She had to fumble all the small change out of her purse. She couldn't count it for the tears that blurred her vision. It was Pearl who gathered up the nickels and pennies, and said as she put the sack in her arms, "There now, toots. I put in five loaves because I know how when there're hungry kids, bread goes like the proverbial snowball in you know where."

Pearl had to open the door for her laden customer, still so blinded by tears, she couldn't find the doorknob.

NINETEEN

The next morning it was Perry McHarg's station wagon which turned off Hubbell Street and headed north toward Bannon. Seated in front with him were Stacy and Jeanie. Stacy wore her long-skirted green print, and Jeanie's ninety-eight pounds were encased in a ribbed brown silk which had once been a Swedish court costume.

"Mom inherited a trunkful of them from a great-aunt. We ripped off tons of braid and it's still heavy," she laughed.

Katie Rose, her poke bonnet in her lavender-sprigged lap and her full skirt tucked in close to keep

255

the littles from mussing it, sat behind with them.

Liz had surprised them all by announcing that morning, "I won't be going to Cherry Day with you. There's a little something I'd like to get settled before I go back to Bannon." And that's all she would answer to their amazed questions. Though she did say to both Jeanie and Katie Rose, "May God keep His hand on your shoulder this day." And she did ask, "What time will you be back?"

"Before eight," Stacy assured her. "Because I promised the Novaks they could leave for their big reunion dance at a quarter to. Because they're meeting old classmates for liquid refreshments en route. But you know how Cherry Day ends at sundown."

Katie Rose explained to Jeanie and Perry McHarg, "That's a traditional hangover from early days. The farmers and their families all had to get home in time to milk the cows—"

"And slop the hogs," added Stacy.

Perry had offered to drive them all in his station wagon when Ben decided to stay home in the hope of being called to work for at least part of the day.

The girls were scooping up their long skirts to climb into the car when the back door banged open on Matt and Brian in bright plaid cowboy shirts that were growing a little small for them. Again Perry said, "I wish you'd look."

"My soul and body!" breathed Stacy.

Katie Rose said quickly, "Don't anybody say a word. Don't anybody even look surprised."

For behind the boys came Jill in the white organdy dress with the appliquéd spray of cherries on the skirt and the bright red bolero jacket. Katie Rose wanted to say, "Oh, let me press it," but she didn't. One shouldn't quibble with miracles.

Looking both defiant and self-conscious, Jill stalked her way to the car and got into the back seat with her brothers and Katie Rose without a word.

"We're off in a cloud of tobacco juice," Perry said. And Katie Rose, to draw attention away from Jill, sang out Bannon's theme song,

> *Come to Bannon on Cherry Day,*
> *Come to Bannon where hearts are gay.*

Brian said, "Remember last year, Katie Rose, when you won a sack of groceries at the grocery booth?"

As though she didn't! That was one of the "ifs" that had kept her awake last night. *If* she won one, it could tide her over maybe a day or two. *If* she didn't, and *if* Grandda gave her a smile, she'd go "yelping for help" to him. But *if* he were still unbending and unforgiving, no choice was left but to accept Rita's offer for the Prom Night wrap.

Perry McHarg was saying to Stacy, "I thought

you'd bring your handsome water-skier with you today."

"Oh no. I know a lot of boys in Bannon," she said happily.

He chuckled. "Like taking a ham sandwich to a banquet, huh?"

The station wagon covered the fifty-seven miles to the little town in fifty minutes. White banners, stretched across the streets, greeted them, WELCOME TO BANNON. WELCOME TO CHERRY DAY.

"Anybody that can drink ten glasses of cherry cider at one time gets a dollar," Matt said.

"Did you ever get the dollar?" Perry asked.

"I purt-near did. I drank eight."

"It don't taste so good after five or six," Brian contributed.

The parade was already forming on the schoolhouse grounds when Perry stopped the car, and they all tumbled out. "I feel practically nude without whiskers," he said, and one of the littles told him, "If you lived here they'd make you pay a fine for not having any."

"There's Grandda—there by the stagecoach," Stacy said. "He's motioning to us. And there's Uncle Tim riding a gray horse."

Uncle Tim, as usual, was dressed as an old-time sheriff with six-guns sagging his holster belt and a very oversized star on his vest glinting in the sun.

"I hope he don't see us," Jill muttered uneasily.

Before the girls could reach the stagecoach, a boy in a wide ten-gallon hat grabbed Stacy by the wrist. "Stacy! Come on and ride in the surrey with me."

So Stacy, poke bonnet in place over her pony tail, climbed into the surrey with the fringe on top, while Katie Rose and Jeanie crowded themselves into the stagecoach with the other passengers.

The Palomino Patrol led the parade. Behind it came the school band.

Come to Bannon where hearts are gay—

Jeanie, looking more dress than girl in her yards of brown silk, leaned over from her seat which faced Katie Rose and said, "Remember what Liz said about a good *forgetter*? Let's work our forgetters all day and just have fun."

Katie Rose nodded. She glanced up at her red-bearded grandfather on the high seat holding in the four mettlesome horses while the phaeton, bearing the visiting governor, Bannon's mayor, and their ladies, swung into position ahead of him.

She craned her neck backward to see the floats which followed. The loveliest, and the one that brought the loudest cheering as it passed by, was the red and white one with the Cherry Queen, all white tulle and red satin ribbons sitting on her throne surrounded by her ladies in waiting. The cherries in the queen's crown were not real, but the ones in the wide basket she held were Bannon's choicest.

"What happened to Perry and the littles?" Jeanie asked as they too waved at the crowd.

"The boys will be riding burros at the tail end of the parade. The last I saw of Jill she was dodging Uncle Tim. I don't know about Perry. He's probably talking to some motel owner about his heating system."

The parade ended at the fairgrounds on the edge of town. Passengers were disgorged at the gate to go through the turnstile, while the vehicles went through the wide gate and to the sheds at the far end. It was just as well Katie Rose hadn't pressed the white organdy Jill wore. She proudly announced she had ridden a Shetland pony right behind the covered wagon.

Grandda assembled the seven from Denver. He paid their admissions, waving aside Perry with, "Don't you know Denver money is no good up here?" He peeled off dollar bills and gave them to the littles, Stacy and Katie Rose, and even thrust one into Jeanie's hand. "For cotton candy or chances on the hope chest."

"I wish I had a grandda like you," Jeanie said gaily.

The man at the turnstile called out, "Hold on to your ticket stubs. You might win a gate prize."

Grandda was gone with the stagecoach.

Red and white booths were thick on the fairgrounds. The P.T.A. pastry booth. The Ladies' Guild needlework booth. The 4-H club was selling hot dogs. The hamburger stand was manned by the Boy Scouts. And freely interspersed were the booths, now completely surrounded, where the thirsty could drink their fill of cherry cider. With every step Katie Rose and Jeanie took, someone was asking, "Would you like to buy a chance on the afghan?" Or the double wedding-ring quilt. Or the patio set. Or the hope chest Grandda thought they'd be interested in. Wouldn't they like to win a Shetland pony so gentle a baby could ride him?

God forbid, Katie Rose thought.

She shook her head to all the questions, her eyes questing through the melee for the grocery booth and its hawkers who cried out, "Five dollar's worth of groceries for one lucky dime. Three tickets for a quarter."

Jeanie sniffed the redolence of frying hamburgers. "Let's buy one."

"I want to use my money for chances on groceries. The cupboard is bare at home."

Jeanie, who today was like the Jeanie of old, said, "We'll use my dollar too, and I've got—oh maybe eighty cents besides."

They didn't go hungry because suddenly two buns,

swaddled in paper napkins, were handed them by a smiling, ruddy-faced man.

Jeanie needed no introduction to him. This was Leo, one of the Callanan relatives who had come in from Bannon last spring to install the Belford bath under the stairs. "I thought you two looked kind of undernourished," he said.

Katie Rose asked him about his wife, Annie, and their new baby. "You'll see them at the picnic supper," he said.

Stacy was suddenly beside them and unceremoniously set her poke bonnet on Jeanie's head. She was now wearing the ten-gallon hat of her surrey companion. "Come on over to the horse corral," she urged. "Duff is going to be in the bronco-busting."

"Maybe later on," Katie Rose said.

Her and Jeanie's way to the grocery booth with its spinning wheel and bulging sacks was again interrupted. "Well, if it isn't Katie Rose! Just when I was wishing I had a pretty girl to give this bottle of perfume to that I won."

The donor had a cheerful boyish face under his balding head. Katie Rose thanked him for the perfume (but she couldn't help wishing it were a ham instead) and introduced Jeanie to Mr. Leffingwell, owner of the Bannon mills. He told Jeanie, "Katie Rose's mother was Cherry Queen when she was about as old as you girls. Prettiest queen Bannon ever had."

He started on, but turned to call back, "Now, Katie Rose, if you folks need anything from the mill, I can easy open up for you."

Jeanie looked after him. "So that's the one that loved your mother when she was a girl—and still does. He's nice."

Katie Rose nodded while she thought: If only Leff knew how sorely the Belfords needed some of his flour and meal.

While they were trying "to beat the wheel" at the grocery booth, different ones of their crowd joined them briefly. Perry McHarg showed them the purple plush panda he had won. Matt brought the information that Uncle Tim wasn't so very mad at them. He had given them a whole book of tickets on the Shetland pony because he was afraid he might win it. Jill pointed out to Katie Rose a boy in a red shirt. "He's the one Matt traded Old Glassy to. And now he just hangs onto it and won't swap it for nothing."

"*Anything*," Katie Rose corrected, her eyes on the spinning wheel. She was holding her last group of three tickets in her hand. One of them was 32. She watched the wheel slowing, slowing— The pointer on it all but stopped at 32. Then with a little shiver and sigh, it moved on to the next number. "Number 8 is the lucky winner," came the loud announcement.

With her own shiver and sigh, Katie Rose tore her tickets into shreds and dropped them on the ground. This was not her lucky day. With another small shiver she looked about for Grandda. She saw him, but he was with the knot of men, including the governor and the mayor, who were walking toward the pavilion.

The day wore on. Everyone had to shout over the visiting band or the Bannon band. The governor gave a short speech from the low bandstand in the pavilion, the mayor a lengthy one.

The Young Democrats and the Young Republicans held their baseball game with good-natured rivalry running high. There were the usual sack and egg races for the young fry, the usual ejection of a quarrelsome drunk by the sheriff, and the usual announcements over the loud-speaker of small children who were lost from parents.

But there was never a chance for Katie Rose to buttonhole Grandda in private.

The rolling out of the keg of beer, and the men in baseball uniforms surrounding it, told when the game was over. The flurry of mothers and their gathering together their broods told when it was time for the picnic supper.

Aunt Kitty caught Katie Rose by the arm with a testy "Oh, here you are." She looked flushed and harried in her long red calico, and she broke into Katie

Rose's introduction of Jeanie with, "See that big table over there under the cottonwood with two baskets and a thermos on it. You two go and hold it down while I round up the clan. Honestly, Da is like the Irishman's flea—now you see him and now you don't. I saw Tim with that nice young man that came with you. Is he your beau, Katie Rose?"

"He's our boarder." And she was planning, *I'll manage to sit next to Grandda at supper.*

The clan finally assembled at the table under the cottonwood. Jeanie whispered, "How do you ever keep track of your relatives? There must be thirty here, Katie Rose."

But there was food enough for twice that many. Great roasters of Aunt Kitty's fried chicken. Annie's meat loaf. Baked beans, foil-wrapped and steaming hot in casseroles. Bowls of potato salad, cole slaw, and great mounds of buttered rolls. Freezers of ice cream, protected from the sun by wet gunny sacks.

Katie Rose glanced at Perry McHarg. She could almost see him thinking, "All home-cooked. No built-in maid service here."

Grandda was the last to arrive. He was at the far end of the table from Katie Rose and—wouldn't you know?—flanked by the same Perry McHarg and Uncle Tim.

Aunt Kitty, who was keeping a watchful eye on

her "one" and the Belford littles, was ordering, "Now eat up, everybody, so we'll be in time for the drawing of the gate prizes. You never saw so many and such expensive prizes—a mink stole and color TV— Did any of you win anything on the raffles?"

Leave it to Jill—organdy dress or no—to spill whatever you didn't want her to. "Katie Rose used up all her money—and Jeanie's too—taking chances on groceries, but she didn't win a thing."

Grandda held his coffee cup poised a minute before he put it down. "Do you all have your gate tickets? You got yours, Katie Rose?"

She pulled it out of the pocket of her sprigged yellow calico. "Mine's easy to remember—916. Because my birthday was the ninth of January and I was sixteen."

Everyone else looked at their numbers and compared them.

Grandda asked Uncle Tim something, and he answered loudly, "Leff? He's right over there—see, eating with the bunch that works at the mill."

Grandda put his plate down. He had a few things he had forgotten to take care of, he said. Perry asked if he needed any help, and Grandda studied him thoughtfully. "Your station wagon is parked right outside the gate, isn't it. Yes—yes, I could use a lift."

"Honestly!" Aunt Kitty scolded as they walked

away. "Da didn't even finish his supper. He seems to think Cherry Day would fall to pieces if he didn't run himself ragged."

Stacy said, "But after all, he's one of the foundling fathers."

"Founding," Katie Rose corrected automatically as she watched her grandfather's long strides. It was no use, she thought drearily. She had cut herself off from him, and he was purposely avoiding her. There was nothing left but to accept Rita's offer for her cherished Prom Night.

Aunt Kitty's voice prodded her, "Katie Rose, don't just sit there mooning. Eat your ice cream."

By now the picnic crowd was drifting toward the bandstand with its protective top against the sun, and the rains that had often descended. All the donated prizes were in full view on the platform. So was the glass fish bowl with its hundreds of tickets matching the stubs which were clutched hopefully in hundreds of hands. The usual fringe of small children sat on the edge of the low bandstand.

The town auctioneer, whom everyone called Sam and who was also Grandda's cement finisher, added a bit of vaudeville to the drawing of the gate prizes. He modeled the mink stole by draping it around his paunchy frame and mincing across the stage in it. He called on one of the small children to reach deep into the fish bowl and, with eyes closed tight, draw a ticket.

The seats were all filled and Katie Rose, standing next to Jeanie at the back, whispered, "I wonder if a person won a prize if she could turn it back for money."

Jeanie grinned in sympathy. "I should think so. Only maybe you'd feel embarrassed for people to know—"

"That I was desperate? Yes, I would because everyone knows us here in Bannon. But look, Jeanie, if by chance they call number 916, I'll quick slip you my ticket—"

"I wouldn't be a bit embarrassed. If I won the stole, I could say I was allergic to mink. If I won the TV, I'd say TV was hard on my eyes."

They needn't have worried. The mink stole went amid much clapping to a schoolteacher. The color TV was next and after it, the movie camera. Because razors hadn't been used for a while or so in Bannon, Sam's quips about the electric razor—and whether or not it had a "mower attachment"—brought loud guffaws.

But none of them, as far as Katie Rose could discern, came from Grandda O'Byrne. She wondered where he was. She began to lose interest when Sam got down to the certificate for a permanent from Bannon's House of Beauty, and another for a lubricating job at the Phillip's Station.

Sam's booming witticisms were interrupted briefly. Someone called to him from behind the tarpaulin curtains in back of the stage. He parted them and bent his bulky figure while he listened and nodded to the unseen interrupter.

"There's only that set of beads and earrings left," a woman near Katie Rose said.

Yes, the drawing for prizes was all but over. And so was Katie Rose's last thin hope. She was about to tear up the ticket in her hand when Sam pounded with his gavel and announced, "Hold on to your tickets, everyone. The show isn't over. As soon as some lucky person wins this handsome set of crystal beads and earrings to wear or give to his sweetie, we still have another prize from an anonymous donor."

Even as the necklace set was drawn for and given away, two men hoisted a huge and heavy carton onto the platform. Every neck craned to see what it was. "No, farmers and gamblers, it's not the Shetland pony," Sam bellowed out. "It's groceries, and if I weren't already stuffed with fried chicken, I'd be drooling."

For this grand finale, said Sam, he would call on the prettiest little doll sitting on the platform edge. He motioned to a tiny blond girl in a pink dress to come and draw out a ticket.

There's no use hoping, Katie Rose told herself and

her pounding heart. But her eyes were riveted on the small hand as it delved into the glass bowl, as it came out with a small stub. The auctioneer took it from her, and his voice thundered out, "The lucky winner and the well-fed person for weeks to come is holding ticket 916."

Katie Rose stood frozen to the spot until Jeanie nudged her, "Yell out, you stupe. That's your number." From Katie Rose came a thin piping sound, "It's me—I've got it—I've got it—" and holding aloft the gray stub, she started through the crowd to the platform.

Sam called out jovially before she reached it, "You'll need some help, little girl child. This carton weighs more than you do."

TWENTY

The western sun was dropping low over Stacy's "Piker's Peak" when Perry McHarg's laden station wagon stopped at the side of the Belford house. Stacy, with a muttered "Oh lawsy me, the Novaks are waiting to take off," was the first one out. Long skirts and all, she went flying across the street to begin her baby-sitting.

Surprisingly enough, the Belford house was empty. Matt ran in to ask Ben to help with the carton of groceries, "He's not home, and neither is Liz," he yelled from the doorway.

Ben must be working late, but where could Liz be?

It took the combined efforts of Perry, Katie Rose, Jeanie, and the littles to carry the huge and heavy box from the car into the kitchen. "Keep a hand on the bottom so it won't give way," Perry kept admonishing.

They all fell to unloading it. They removed the top layer of cherry pies and homemade bread and set them on the table. Next came tomatoes, carrots, cabbage. "Hand me everything that goes in the refrigerator," Katie Rose said.

Never had a slab of bacon or unwieldy ham looked so beautiful. Each stewing hen or fryer, frozen stiff as granite from its stay in a locker, she handled lovingly. She had to take out ice-cube trays to make room for the roasts.

No wonder it had taken all six of them to tussle the big carton in! Its bottom layer had come from the Bannon mills. Four sacks of flour and meal were wedged in tight.

The ham was too large to fit in the refrigerator. With much scampering about, the littles found the meat saw and Perry cut and sawed it into pieces. He looked at the clock then, and said, "I guess you can manage now, Katie Rose. I want to see the pastry cook at the Golden Slipper."

The littles also took off to tell the glad tidings of Katie Rose's winning. Only Katie Rose and Jeanie were left with all the disarray in the kitchen.

Katie Rose let her eyes feast on the piled-high dinette table. This wasn't gloating as she had that Saturday morning when she filled cupboards and refrigerator with all her cans and neat packages from the Maplewood Mart. This feeling went deeper. For she had known the panic, the near terror of no food in the house and a hungry family to feed. This was prayerful gratitude.

"Now Rita Flood can't get her greedy little mitts on my Prom Night wrap," she breathed out.

"Rita Flood?"

"I had to sell her my fashion-show dress yesterday—"

"Oh no!"

She told a sympathetic Jeanie of that haggling scene, and Jeanie was just saying, "I didn't know you were that pushed, Katie Rose," when the front door opened.

They expected to see Ben, but it was Liz and Jeanie's mother who came in. Jeanie said in surprise, "Why, Mom, how'd you know I needed a ride home?"

Katie Rose gestured toward the foodstuffs and said joyfully, "Look, Liz—just look, Mrs. Kincaid, what I won." She launched into a dramatic recounting of her last-minute stroke of luck in winning the carton of groceries. The two listened, but Katie Rose had a feeling they were giving her wondrous news only divided attention. They both had a flushed, excited air like two conspirators who had shared an adventure.

Jeanie too noticed it, and interrupted Katie Rose's recital to ask, "What have you two been up to?" And Katie Rose, who reached out to close a dinette window, suddenly exclaimed, "Liz, where is your box of pansies?"

"Jeanie's mother and I took them back to the woman who threw them."

"You what?" Jeanie asked in a shocked voice.

"That's right," Liz said. "I was curious—just plain curious—about why that woman went scuttling out of Wetzel's store as you said she did when Dr. Kincaid was mentioned. And why she'd go banging that box of flowers at Miguel's camera and then streak off like a scalded cat—"

Jeanie's horrified eyes turned from her to her mother. "And *you* went with her?"

Her mother nodded. "Liz planned to have Ben take her, but he got a call to go to work—"

"And didn't know when he'd get back—it was some sort of emergency about a bridge approach," Liz added easily. "So your mother and I decided to go when she finished at Mount Carmel."

Jeanie's tortured eyes went from one to the other. "Well, did you present her with her pansies—and did you find out what you wanted to know?" she demanded harshly. "I wish you'd kept your noses out of it."

Her mother said suddenly, "Jeanie, do you remember the nurse—her name was Miss Matson—that took care of you that time you got so sick on your birthday? The time when I came down with a virus at the same time? Maybe you don't remember her—because you were pretty sick—"

"I remember her letting the vapor teakettle boil dry so that the spout dropped off. And I remember— or maybe I've just heard you tell it—about Dad raking her over the coals over the medicine she gave me. Why? Why are you asking me now?"

"Because your pansy-throwing woman is that terrible snippy, man-crazy nurse we had ten years ago."

Jeanie in her long and weighty brown silk, and looking like a little girl dressed in her mother's clothes, only stared first at one and then another vacantly. "But I don't see why a nurse—would throw something at me—"

"Her name is Marlene Matson," Liz said. " 'Little Marlie,' Walt called her. Maybe the two of us aren't making much sense. Start from the first, Mrs. Kincaid, and tell her the way you told it to me."

"Jeanie, listen. You remember ten years ago when we were going to have your birthday party? And how that morning I decorated your cake and washed your hair? I doubt if your wet hair had anything to do with your getting sick, except that I always connect them in my mind. Your temperature started going up, and we had to call off your party. And before I'd phoned the last little girl, I was headachy and dizzy myself—"

"But I still don't see—"

"Let me go on. Because there was such an epidemic of whatever virus it was, the hospitals were full. Your father tried to get one of the nurses he knew to come in and take care of us but—there again—nurses were hard to get. He got one from the Nurses' Registry and, as we realized afterward, we must have gotten the bottom of the heap. She was a pert, flighty little thing, not long out of training—"

"And she hasn't changed except for the worse," Liz put in.

Mrs. Kincaid gave Jeanie her grave and loving smile. "It was the infection in your Eustachian tube that your father was so worried about. He left the nurse sedative tablets to ease the pain in your ear. She was to give you *half* a tablet. Leave it to your dad to count the tablets and find she'd given you far more than his prescribed dosage! She hadn't bothered to cut them in half. She had kept you doped with them so you wouldn't be any trouble for her, I suppose—"

"And so she could talk for hours on the phone,"

Jeanie said, her face puckered in memory. "She'd pull the phone in my room and talk on and on. I remember asking her for a drink, and she'd motion me to keep still—"

"Talking to that man she was carrying on with," Liz tch-tched. "And letting you go thirsty, the heartless strumpet."

"She was crazy about an orderly at one of the hospitals," Mrs. Kincaid went on. "Remember, Jeanie, how our house on Downing was only two blocks from the drugstore? I realized afterwards she was running out and meeting him there. That's how the vapor kettle boiled dry. That's why she kept you doped up maybe—and that's what your father hit the ceiling about—"

Katie Rose asked, "What'd she say when he did?"

"I don't know. He fired her and wrote out a check for her two days. He told her he was reporting her to the Registry for malpractice."

"So that's why she was so shaken-up when Mr. Wetzel said Dr. Kincaid might stop in to get his cheese," Katie Rose said.

"That's not the whole *why* of it," Mrs. Kincaid said on a twisted smile. "When our canceled checks came back at the end of the month, what do you suppose we found? That she had raised the doctor's check a *hundred* dollars. It wasn't even a good job of forgery, but it went through. She passed it to a used-car dealer for a car for her and the orderly to drive to Arizona. Some day, Jeanie, when I can put my hand on it, I'll show you the check."

Jeanie still seemed to have trouble adjusting or perhaps dislodging certain fixed ideas. She seemed incapable of asking questions.

But Katie Rose wasn't. "So you two drove all the way out to Pinhorn Road. Did you have trouble finding her?"

"Indeed we did," Liz said. "We covered a good part of Colorado before we found the white house where her uncle lives. She wasn't there. Those pansies weren't hers at all, I'll have you know. He had given her the money to get them to put in his porch box. We gave them back to him."

"I was able to piece the story together when we talked to him," Mrs. Kincaid said, and again that half-guilty and amused look passed between her and Liz, "but just for the pure heck of it, we decided to go on to the Little Shoe Tavern and see the one-time Miss Matson in person."

"You did? You two went into that bar?" Katie Rose exclaimed.

"And why not?" said Liz. "Sure, we're both over-age."

Jeanie came out of her bewildered silence to say,

"Why did you go there if you already knew who she was?"

"We wanted to give her a bad time," Liz admitted. "And I wanted to see her face when she looked up and saw your mother. We saw her in the booth, far gone in whatever she was drinking and"—she gave a roguish chortle—"we waited till the barkeep cleared off their empty glasses and before he'd time to bring full ones—that was in case she'd feel like throwing something—and then we walked up, big as life, and your mother said, 'How are you, Miss Matson? I'm Mrs. Kincaid—Dr. Kincaid's wife.'"

"I'd have liked to have been there," Katie Rose said. "Did she say anything?"

"She wasn't capable of saying much. She hunched in her corner like a scared rabbit."

"Was she there with that Walt?" Katie Rose asked. "And did he say to let the dead past bury its dead?"

"Ah yes, the same Walt—and him braying like a donkey, and insisting we sit down and have a beer. And we did—only we paid for our own ginger beer. And I must say it didn't taste like any I've tasted in the old days. I was minded to ask the fellow behind the bar if they dipped it out of Little Shoe Creek."

Jeanie said in a wondering voice, "So that's how she knew when my birthday was—because she came the day I was to have the party. That's why she remembered." Her face was suddenly luminous as though a light had been turned on in all the dark doubting corners of her mind and heart. And then tears rolled down her cheeks.

Again Katie Rose looked at her in amazement just as she had when she had laughed so wildly outside the Little Shoe Tavern. But again she remembered; Blake had not only written about excess of sorrow laughing, but "Excess of joy weeps."

Mrs. Kincaid said on a flash of gray eyes, "I should think she would remember your birthday! She ate every bite of your birthday cake—though she probably fed her orderly some of it."

Liz said with relish, "I doubt if 'poor little Marlie' will be sponging off her old uncle much longer. I think your telling her that you'd turned the forged check over to the D.A.—"

"That wasn't true of course," Mrs. Kincaid said on a rueful laugh. "We kissed that hundred dollars good-by ten years ago. I just threw that in for good measure to make her squirm."

Liz went on with even more relish, "And there we sat drinking our ginger beer and enjoying all her cringing and her muttering excuses and promises. But it was pitiful too, seeing a poor thing like that with no home, no roots, no memories to hold to, and nothing much to look forward to."

"Jeanie and I thought maybe she'd marry Walt," Katie Rose said.

"Then you can think again," Liz said shortly. "Walt already has a wife back in Iowa taking care of her sick mother."

"How did you find out?"

"I asked him," Liz said simply.

And then any doubts Katie Rose had as to whether these two women knew the nightmare Jeanie had been going through were dispelled. Mrs. Kincaid pushed the heavy hair back from Jeanie's tearful face and chided, "Jeanie—oh, Jeanie, honey, why didn't you tell us what you were tormenting yourself about? What are mothers and fathers for? You needn't have suffered so. One look at her—bleached hair or no—and I could have told you—"

"It's all right now," Jeanie said. "Everything's all right now. It doesn't matter—I mean, it doesn't matter who my mother was—or wasn't. I wonder why I ever thought it did, when I've got you and Dad. Let's go home, Mom." She said it like a child who has been lost in the dark and taken strange and frightening turns. "I feel as though I'd been away for so long."

TWENTY-ONE

A lashing rain came down in the night.

Katie Rose was wakened by damp gusts driving through the window, and got up to close it. She snuggled down again by the warm lump that was Jill, and her first sleep-befogged thought was: Jill hasn't grumbled a grumble lately about wearing those ruffly baby doll pajamas.

She thought then of Jeanie. Poor little Jeanie so devastated by the thought that the shoddy, shrill-voiced woman could be her mother. But now Jeanie would be her old twinkling-eyed, predictable self again. Ah, Liz was the sly one. She had heard Jeanie's an-

guished outburst that day they came back from Pinhorn Road and the Little Shoe Tavern. It was more
than curiosity that kept Liz from going to Cherry
Day. She couldn't bear to leave Jeanie in the nightmare of her own imagining.

Katie Rose's last lovely picture before she fell asleep
again was of the full refrigerator. Thanks to a benevolent fate, she had been saved from humbling herself
to Grandda. And saved from the humiliation of giving
Rita Flood possession of the Prom Night wrap she,
Katie Rose, was so proud of and loved so.

The rain was still falling the next morning. The
family delayed their going to Mass because of it. They
went at noon when the downpour had settled to a
drizzle.

Liz lost no time when they came home in putting
the butt end of ham on to cook. From upstairs came
the clickety-clack of Perry McHarg's typewriter.

"He has a few papers to finish," Liz told Katie Rose.
"He says he has till tomorrow to turn them in."

"Did he say when he was leaving?"

"He may leave today if he can wind them up."

And then the house was suddenly full of bustling
activity. Grandda phoned from Bannon. He told Ben
of the telegram he had received from Gran. The travelers had already reached New York, and would be arriving on Flight 102 at the airport a little after five.

Grandda said, "I'll drive down and meet them at the airport. You folks stay home and get ready for them—you know how neither your mother or Gran like greetings or good-bys in public. I checked to be sure, and there's no dinner served on that flight."

"Ah, that'll be nice," Liz said when Ben relayed the message. "They'll be home in time for a good hot supper. And I'll have all my bits and pieces packed so I can go back to Bannon with the folks afterwards."

Katie Rose looked at her rosy, benign face. She hadn't a doubt now that when Liz heard of Mother's going to Ireland she had said to herself—or maybe to Gran and Grandda—"I'll go in and mother them as best I can while their own mother's gone."

"We'll miss you a lot, Liz." They would all miss her kindly wisdom, her "May God sleep on your pillow" when she told them goodnight.

"We hate to see you go," Katie Rose said.

"Life is full of comings and goings, dear heart."

But Katie Rose had mixed feelings about the other departer. The typewriter was stilled now, but there was much stirring about in the room she had made ready for him. The boarder she had gone to such pains to impress! Well, she had, she thought wryly. No doubt, she had served as the Horrible Example for his paper on "Getting the Most out of Your Food Dollar."

By late afternoon the house was shining for Mother's

homecoming. Every time Katie Rose stepped into the dinette she bumped into the huge carton that sat there. It still held the sacks of flour. Katie Rose debated over them. The new bath under the stairs had deprived the kitchen of some of its cupboard space. What else could one do with those sacks but let them sit against the dinette wall? But now, after her panicky days of no food, they seemed less offensive than before.

She lifted them out. She dragged the carton out the back door to tear apart and burn in the ashpit. The drizzle had changed to a fine mist. The unwieldy carton was built of sturdy, reinforced cardboard. It was all she could do to rip it apart and jam the pieces into the round opening of the ashpit. She lit a match to the pieces.

The bottom of the carton was a solid piece. It was too wide to go in, and too heavy to rip apart or bend. She was pondering as she turned it over whether to go back to the kitchen for a knife to slash through it—

And that's when she saw the address label. That's when she realized that what had been the bottom of the loaded carton was really the top which bore the name of the person who had received it. She stood and stared at the heavy black letters, URBAN J. O'BYRNE, BANNON, COLORADO.

Urban J. O'Byrne? Strange, that her prize-winning carton of groceries should have Grandda's name on it! Or—was—it—so—strange? Her heart began a slow hard beating. And with each thump, she was seeing—yes, and hearing—small details that fitted into a picture.

Grandda's absorbed look when Jill said that Katie Rose and Jeanie had spent all their money trying to win a sack of groceries. He had put down his coffee cup. He said he had forgotten to tend to something. And when old Hawk-eye McHarg asked if he needed any help, he said yes, that he could use his station wagon.

She stood on quite unmindful of the misty drizzle reaching through to her scalp. She was picturing Sam on the bandstand, and the interrupting of his gay patter and the drawing of ticket stubs. He had parted the tarpaulin at the back of the platform and bent over to talk and nod understandingly to whoever had called him. She heard again the rap of his gavel as he announced that there was to be a final gate prize by an *anonymous* donor—

But how could that tiny blond girl have drawn ticket number 916 so fortuitously? A laugh that was more of a grunt escaped Katie Rose. The little girl hadn't. She had merely drawn *a* number and handed it to Sam. And he, without even putting on his glasses, had bellowed out the number he had been coached in.

What a hurried scramble Grandda must have had

to assemble the contents of the box! He had sought out the obliging Leff first to rush down and open the Bannon mill. (She remembered his asking Uncle Tim if he had seen Leff.) Then Grandda had gone to the freezer plant and pilfered his own locker for the meats. Back at the fairgrounds he had probably said to his accomplice, Perry McHarg, "You get pies and bread at the Pastry Booth—just tell them they're for Urban O'Byrne—while I scoop up some vegetables from the Farm Display."

So it hadn't been a benevolent fate that rescued Katie Rose after all!

The back door opened, and Perry McHarg came out with a suitcase in one hand and in the other a full wastebasket which he set on the ground. Behind him came Matt and Brian, also laden with luggage. Katie Rose watched with baleful eyes while he loaded his station wagon at the curb. She watched him say good-by to the boys and, walking back, pick up the wastebasket. He carried it through the dark gray day to the ashpit and her at the back of the lot.

"I'll add something to your conflagration," he said cheerily, "and then tell you good-by."

She had no answering smile. "You told Grandda I was out of food, didn't you?"

He looked at her grim face, and then at the big square carton top in her hand with the address on it.

She added bitterly, "I'd have told him myself if I'd had half a chance. But I suppose you couldn't wait to get to Bannon and go blabbing that I—I—"

"I did not blab, Katie Rose," he said quietly.

"Then Stacy—or one of the littles—"

But even as she said it, she remembered back to Friday morning when Grandda had stopped in while she was in the basement taking bleak stock of her situation.

Liz had told her she had given him coffee. Grandda always took cream in it. He must have opened the refrigerator to get some—she had seen him do it often. One glance would reveal its stark emptiness. Oh, and her list—her meager list! She had left it on the dinette table. Perhaps Jill's remark about her spending her money for grocery chances had only reminded him of it.

Katie Rose said in a voice as sodden as the ground she stood on, "All right, go ahead and crow. Go ahead and say I told you so. I'm sure you'll get A plus on your marketing piece with me as the Horrible Example. I can even give you some swell titles for it—*Tenderloin Tips Were Her Undoing, or Miss Idiot of the Year Saved by Her Grandfather's Charity*. All that malarky—about the anonymous donor—" she began to cry, "—was just his way—of saving face—for me—"

He shook her arm. "Listen, Katie Rose. It was saving face for him too. As I get it, he had flown off the handle with you—"

"Yes, he said hell would freeze over—" she gulped out, "before he'd give me—so much as a—a banty egg. And he doesn't call me blackbird any more. I hurt his feelings—and I'm sorry—"

He chuckled. "I think he's sorry for what he said too. Anyway, let's just say it was the only way one hot-headed, stiff-necked O'Byrne knew to help another hot-headed, stiff-necked one."

A slow smile tugged at her lips. "I guess you're right. He didn't want to come right out and say, 'I didn't mean that about your not coming yelping to me for help.' So he said it with cabbage and cornmeal and a slab of bacon." The weight lifted from her heart.

They stood on by the smoking ashpit. He took the carton top from her, whacked it over his knee and put the bent pieces in the fire. "If I were you, Katie Rose, I wouldn't make any to-do about it to your grandfather. Sometimes people say too much. I've sure kicked myself for going at you so roughshod at the supermarket that day. I don't wonder you got your back up."

"Mom always says I have to learn everything the hard way." She added in a defeated voice, "I know you'll think I'm crazy, Perry, but ever since Mom left I've had the dream of her and Gran coming home, and

all of us sitting at the table with the flowers and candles and amber glasses—all so different from the way it
was before. But it won't be that way now. Liz is boiling the ham, and she'll put cabbage and potatoes with
it. I saw them on the drainboard. And I haven't the
heart to say I want to do it my way, because I've been
such a big, fat flop."

"You have not been a big, fat flop. And when you
go back in the house you'll find out."

"What'll I find?"

He laughed. "For one thing Jill stopped me at the
head of the stairs and asked me if I thought the dress
she wore yesterday needed ironing—she didn't say
pressing. And I told her yes. So you may see her
whisking an iron over it. And Liz whispered to me
that she couldn't wait to see your mother's face when
she saw Jill in a dress. 'Katie Rose has worked a miracle,' she said."

"You helped on the miracle. That is, your coming
separated Jill from the boys and got her in my room.
Do you have to leave right away, Perry? Can't you
stay and meet Mom?"

"I'd like to. But I want to clock off the miles this
evening so I can make it to Phoenix by noon tomorrow."

There was something she had to know. She blurted
out, "Perry, why did you call up and ask if you could

come to our house? I mean, there's a long list of boarding places—"

"I called because I couldn't forget you. Don't hate me, but I had a sort of fatherly feeling of wanting to protect you. I've never had it with a girl before. That first evening I listened to you babbling happily about following the McHarg menus, and I thought of the hungry tribe you'd have to feed. I had only been at the McHargs a week when I realized how much more Carol paid out for all that fancy ready-to-eat food than if she reached for a stewing pot herself. Like I say, Katie Rose, I'm the rooted-to-the-ground type. But you fly high on wings—and I didn't want to see them bruised."

So now she knew. But she felt no wounding of feminine vanity. It flashed through her mind that relationships between the opposite sexes could be comfortable—even special—without infatuation or romance. I've learned a lot in this new and different summer, she thought.

Perry said musingly, "We meet some people in life, and it's like ships passing in the night. You meet others—and they leave a dent on you, so that you're a little different person when you say good-by."

"Did I leave a dent on you?" she asked soberly.

"Quite a dent. From now on I'll be looking for your shine and stubbornness—and your big heart—in every girl I meet." He laughed softly, "I'll even ask myself: Would this girl track down mice for her young brother? Would she buy red rugs for my room when she couldn't afford it? Does she dance like a will-of-the-wisp?" He reached out and took both her hands. "We're not enemies now, are we?"

"No, we're not enemies—and I'm glad."

"Good-by, Katie Rose." He pulled her closer and kissed her lightly on her cheek. "You're a sweet kid. Now skeedaddle in the house before you get any wetter."

"Good-by, Hawk-eye McHarg. You left a big dent on me, too."

They waved to each other as he turned onto Hubbell Street.

Liz was waiting for her in the kitchen door. "We'll be seeing him again one of these days. But you'd better be grinding the ham, lovey. I wasn't sure whether you used the coarse or fine blade."

"What do you mean—*grind* the ham?" Katie Rose asked.

"For your ham timbales. We don't want to give these folks boiled ham and cabbage. Unless things have changed a lot over in County Cork, they've had their fill of it. And I picked out the nicest tomatoes for you to scoop out and fill with that cabbage salad you made one night. It looked so pretty. Yes, your mother and Gran have had all these weeks of plain Irish food. So let's have no boiled potatoes. I wondered, now that we've plenty of shortening, if we couldn't be making french fries."

Katie Rose stared at her in wonder, and Liz added gently, "Ah, sweetling, life is full too of making the most of what you have to do with. We used to say along the river Lee, 'Weave your kilt according to the wool from your sheep.' It was a foolish woman who fretted herself because her pile of wool was lower than her neighbor's."

"But supposing she didn't have very much wool? Wouldn't she have a pretty skimpy kilt?"

"Indeed not! By maneuvering a bit and piecing in— and maybe foregoing a pleat or two—she'd come out with a lovely prideful one."

A thoughtful Katie Rose tightened the clamp on the meat grinder. Why, Liz was really saying that Katie Rose could follow the *niceness* of the McHarg house-hold even though the Belford budget was lower. And that she needn't fret herself if she had to forego a pleat or two—such as a fruit centerpiece on the sideboard and those Belford mansion teas.

The slam of the side door announced Stacy's arrival. Her reddish hair was darkened by the misty rain, her cheeks were bright, and she carried a handful of roses. "I talked the Novaks out of these late-blooming something-or-others for the table. So let me fix the center-piece, Katie Rose."

"We already set the table," the littles announced, and Matt put in, "It's my turn to light the candles."

Katie Rose glanced at the table in the dining room. The place mats, the amber plates and glasses were all in place. She looked at the scrubbed faces of the boys, and at the brush marks in Jill's hair. Jill was less defiant and self-conscious in her full-skirted white dress today.

"I didn't know you littles—I mean, I didn't think you cared much about having candles on the table."

"Matt fought a kid about it," Jill said. "We told him we had them on the table every night, and he said we were lying. He said nobody ever had candles on the table except on a birthday."

"It was one of the Flood kids that lives next to Wetzel's," Brian contributed.

Ben called out from the dining room, "Get in here, you littles, and put the spoon on the side of the plate with the knife."

So the family liked what they had first scoffed at as Katie Rose's hifalutin ways! Then she hadn't been a big, fat flop after all.

By five o'clock all was in readiness. The timbales and french fries waited in a slow oven. In case the mushroom sauce for the timbales thickened, it could be thinned with Bannon cream. On the table the red of the stuffed tomatoes vied with the red of the roses.

Katie Rose answered the ringing telephone. It was Grandda at the airport telling her that Flight 102 was thirty minutes late. "Seems they had a cloudburst in Chicago that delayed the take-off."

"Dinner will keep. Now don't be hurrying Gran off, Grandda, because we've got places set for all of you."

"That's good. I'm hungry for a woman's cooking." He added on a hearty laugh, "If I know Ireland, they'll both be waterlogged with tea, but haven't had a good cup of coffee since they put foot on the sod. So have a pot of coffee ready, blackbird."

He had called her *blackbird*. "I'll put it on right now," she promised.

And that's when she found they were out of coffee.

But it wasn't as hard as she thought it would be to confess to Ben and Liz and Stacy, "I've spent all the housekeeping money. I haven't a cent to buy coffee at Wetzel's."

Before Ben could reach in his pocket, Stacy said, "No, I've got it. Mr. Novak paid me just now for last night, and I promised Katie Rose she could have all or part of it."

Ben didn't turn his dark accusing look on her. He only said, "I had a feeling we were living too high on the hog for your money to hold out."

"I'll know better next time. I'm scared to think of what Mom will say when she finds out."

Liz made a clucking sound. "You needn't be. I know what she'll say—I've heard her say it often. That nothing involving money is tragic. You'd better get the coffee, lovey."

Before Katie Rose left she phoned Jeanie to tell her of the plane's delay. "I'm dashing down to Wetzel's. There's so much to talk about. Do you need anything from there?"

Yes, her mother thought it'd be nice if they got some Liederkranz cheese for her dad. "I'm on my way," Jeanie sang out.

Katie Rose, coming from Hodgepodge Hollow to the west, and Jeanie, coming from Harmony Heights to the east, met at the steps of the store. They sought the shelter of the porch out of the drizzle.

Katie Rose said first, "I'm dying to know. Did you tell your father about the dog-burger, pansy-throwing, check-raising woman and did he—"

"He came home late and dog-tired last night. I asked Mom not to tell him—not yet. You know, I'm kind of ashamed of the way I went off so half-cocked. Wasn't I the conclusion-jumper? And I'm ashamed of thinking Mom cooked up the story about that rainy morning at Mount Carmel. It's been such a come-to-realize time for me—"

"Such as?"

"Such as that whatever happened before a baby is adopted by parents that love it *is* a closed book—just like the books always say. I've come to realize how lucky I am. Katie Rose, don't you ever let me crab my head off about Dad saying no when I want him to say yes. Because that's another come-to-realize—that he's strict with me because he's built that way. He is with the people who work for him at the clinic, and they look up to him and love him for always being fair. Yes, sir, whenever I start griping, you remind me of his jumping on the nurse for giving me double doses of whatever it was to make me sleep."

"You aren't the only one who's had a come-to-realize summer. If I ever start griping about sour cream in a Mason jar, you remind me of how I had to sell my fashion-show dress to Rita because I—"

"I'd never do that," Jeanie looked toward the unkempt habitat of the Floods next door. "It grieves me so to think you had to. Won't it just rub you raw to see her preening herself in it? It will me."

"Ye-es, but at least she didn't get my Aunt Eustace Prom Night. I know somebody she'd better not do too much preening in front of. Stacy. I haven't told her yet. Stacy and Rita used to have knockdown and drag-outs—with Stacy doing the dragging out."

She told Jeanie then of her discovery that it was not

fate but Grandda who had saved the day for her with the carton of groceries—

"He did! He's a sweetheart."

"And he called me blackbird over the phone. And what do you think? Liz was the one who wanted me to make ham timbales, and the littles set the table, and Stacy rustled up flowers."

"So your dream is coming true after all. Of your mother coming home and being overwhelmed by your new Katie Rose–Mrs. McHarg regime."

Katie Rose's smile was rueful. "Yes, except that in my dream I was sitting there thinking, 'See how smart I am. See how I can run a house better than you, Mom.' I won't be thinking that now. I'll be thinking how well she did—"

"She'll like the changes."

"Yes, I've put out her turquoise blue bath set—Mom always liked pretty things. And when we were grinding the ham, Liz said something about how older folks needed to learn from the young—"

Jeanie giggled. "Did you say that when we young ones got ourselves in a jam it took the older ones to get us out? Remember that windy day when school was almost out—it was only about six weeks ago, but it seems a lifetime—when we stood right here, and wished we could do away with grownups meddling in our lives? We thought we could do so well without them. It was Dad's saying no to me, and spray starch that started us—"

"That reminds me—the coffee. Just when everything was ready, we found we didn't have coffee."

Jeanie lifted her eyebrows primly. "Why, goose girl, I'm surprised at you. Don't you know that Mrs. McHarg never runs out of anything? When *she* finds she's getting low on any foodstuff, *she* puts it on her shopping list."

"Oh hush!"

They laughed together as they opened the door and heard the tinkle of the bell announcing their presence in the little store that had been made over from a house, and smelled of dill pickles, strong cheese, and overripe bananas.

ABOUT THE AUTHOR

Lenora Mattingly Weber was the author of more than twenty-two books for young readers, including the popular Beany Malone series. Beany Malone was the first of Mrs. Weber's heroines, but when she finally married the boy next door in *Something Borrowed, Something Blue,* Mrs. Weber introduced Katie Rose Belford and, later, Katie Rose's sister Stacy, the heroine of her final novels *Hello, My Love, Good-Bye* and *Sometimes a Stranger.*

Lenora Mattingly Weber was born in Missouri, but her family left the state when she was twelve to homestead on the Colorado plains. She went to high school in Denver and after graduation married and lived in Denver. Until her death, in January 1971, Mrs. Weber conducted a monthly column in *Extension Magazine* and wrote short stories for America's leading magazines: *The Saturday Evening Post, Ladies' Home Journal, Good Housekeeping,* and *McCall's,* in addition to her writing for young people.

All of Mrs. Weber's manuscripts and papers and copies of the first editions of each of her books were presented to the Denver Public Library in a ceremony in her honor in November 1969. They are now part of the Colorado Authors Collection in the Western History Department of the library.